York

I0457430

The Vorge Crew – Book Three

By Laurann Dohner

York by Laurann Dohner

Watching his crewmates fall in love has left York craving a female of his own. That's how he ends up being matched to a Parri female through a service to find bond mates. He's excited at the prospect when he arrives on planet Relon. Until he actually meets her.

Betrayed by her government in a bid for alien technology, poverty-stricken human Sara is doomed to be a prince's sex toy, until she's rescued on a planet that doesn't take kindly to slavers. Suddenly free, she's an outcast on her new home, treated with distrust...by everyone except a gorgeous, kind, huge blue alien. Too bad he's getting married the next day. His future bond mate is a horrid, abusive woman, and Sara has a way to save them both—she'll convince York to bond with   her   instead.

The Vorge Crew Series List

Cathian

Dovis

York

York by Laurann Dohner

Copyright © October 2018

Editor: Kelli Collins

Cover Art: Dar Albert

ISBN: 978-1-944526-97-9

York – The Vorge Crew – Book Three

By Laurann Dohner

Prologue

Two weeks prior – Earth

Sara was drowning in fear, betrayal, and most of all, shock. Her stomach heaved but at least she didn't throw up.

One of the women broke loose from where they stood huddled together and made a desperate dash toward a door on the far side of the building.

Two muscled military men rushed after her, grabbing her arms. She screamed and flailed, trying to break free.

A third man in a white coat rushed toward them and jabbed her arm with a syringe. It knocked out the woman fast, and they dragged her limp body away.

That caused a few other women to panic and make a run for it. They didn't make it far. They were captured and drugged, too.

"Remain calm!"

Sara stared at the old jerk yelling behind the podium. He wore a military uniform with some medals attached. A feeling of hopelessness settled in. Even if she were to run and somehow manage to escape the building where they'd been taken, there would be nowhere to go. The police themselves had collected her from her secretary job.

It wasn't a group of criminals who'd stolen her and nineteen other women from their lives. This was a government-sanctioned so-called "program."

She'd heard every word the jerk said to explain why they'd been taken from their lives. He'd even shown a few charts on a big screen behind him, as if graphs could somehow make sense of what he was condoning. Women outnumbered men eight to one. Overpopulation had caused massive food and housing shortages. He'd sworn it would only get worse—but they'd come up with a solution.

"Listen to me," the jerk yelled. "You're doing your country and planet a great service." He cleared his throat, lowering his voice to a normal tone before once more speaking into the microphone. "These aliens will marry you. You won't be harmed. In exchange, we'll receive the technology we desperately need to fix our current problems." A smug expression came over his wrinkled features. "You should feel honored that you've been chosen to represent the best our planet has to offer."

Sara mentally called bullshit. Oh, they might be trading women for technology, but she'd noticed all the other women who'd been brought in were like her—from the poor district. All of them wore similar low-quality clothing, shoddy shoes...

They had been picked because, on Earth, no one cared what happened to them.

Sara glanced at the woman softly crying next to her. "Do you have any family?"

The brunette sniffed and shook her head.

"I don't either," a woman behind them whispered.

Just what Sara figured. No one to miss them or raise hell. Her job had probably already replaced her in the hours since she'd been escorted from the buildings. Jobs were scarce, especially in her district. She'd been one of the lucky ones, able to feed herself and pay rent on a crappy, tiny apartment.

"Let's go. This way," another man shouted.

Sara and the women who hadn't panicked were led to a door at the back. The sun had gone down in the time since they'd arrived.

The sight that met them made her whimper.

A large cargo shuttle waited—and six huge aliens stood at the bottom of a ramp.

Sara had seen aliens on the news a few times, but in person they were even scarier.

These beings had bodies that resembled those of humans but their faces were almost fishlike in shape, with large guppy mouths, and instead of hair, they had large fins running along the backs of their heads.

One of the women in front of her broke into sobs and a guard shoved her forward when she stopped. Sara managed to keep walking. But the urge to flee was strong.

The aliens had devices around their throats, just above their blue inform collars, and she figured out what they were for when one of them spoke. His voice came from the device, rather than his moving mouth.

"Board now. No fighting or you regret."

A shudder ran down her spine as she was herded aboard. There were cages waiting inside. Each woman was shoved into her own. The cages weren't big, only four feet wide, maybe five deep, and about six feet tall. An alien slammed the door, locking her in. He stared at her with big watery yellow eyes and made a gurgling sound, maybe laughter, if she were to guess.

"They tell you to be brides. Lies."

She stepped back. "What do you mean, lie? We're being married off."

That gurgling came again. "Sex slaves," the computerized voice stated from the device at his throat. "Auction take place while we transport and deliver you to buyer at trading planets."

She felt like she was about to throw up again.

The alien moved away, probably informing the other women as he stopped at each of the cages. It seemed to amuse him to see their reactions. A woman down the line from Sara began to shriek.

Sara sat on the hard floor. There wasn't a seat, a blanket, anything...and as she studied the space, she was pretty sure the six-inch drain in the corner passed for a bathroom.

"Oh God," she whispered, hugging her chest tight, the beginnings of tears sliding down her cheeks.

The shuttle took off, and she had to grab hold of the bars when it began to shake violently. Then she *did* get sick, using the hole to empty her breakfast into. Once the ride smoothed out, another alien, this one wearing a holster around his middle, stopped outside of her cage, watching as she wiped her mouth.

"Stand and face."

She hesitated.

He pulled a metal stick off the holster, waving it. It reminded her of a small version of a cattle prod that she'd seen in movies. His words verified her guess. "I touch you with. It hurt. Get up!"

She struggled to her feet and stared at him.

He put the stick back into the holster and pulled out what looked similar to an Earth camera. "Smile for buyers."

She forced one, too afraid to refuse. He scanned up and down her body before turning away. She retook her seat and leaned against the bars, terrified.

It didn't come as a surprise that they'd been lied to, but that whole spiel about being married to respectable aliens who'd treat them well had been her only comfort. That was gone.

"This is so fucked up," a tall blonde in the next cage whispered.

Sara looked at her, nodding.

"No talking!" An alien lunged at the cage holding the blonde and shoved his stick between the bars.

The blonde screamed when it touched her and passed out in seconds.

Sara quickly scooted away from the bars to the back of the cage, sealing her lips tight. The alien stopped in front of her, his yellow eyes fixed on her. "In week, we drop you at trading spot. Buyer pick up and take you home to his world, wherever it be. No talk. No cry. No annoy!"

She managed to nod.

He walked down the row of cages, and Sara silently let the tears fall.

Sometime later, another shuttle met with theirs. Most of the cages with women were taken away, leaving only Sara and one other captive. Most of the fish aliens left with the others, leaving two behind to guard Sara and the other woman. These guards didn't watch over them, instead leaving them to go to the front of the shuttle for hours.

Sara tried to talk to the woman but she seemed to be in a state of deep depression, based on the way she was crying.

"It's going to be okay," she called out to her. "We humans are tough!" She wasn't sure who she was trying to convince more. Herself or the other woman.

She eventually went to sleep curled up on the floor and woke sometime later to one of the guards yelling.

Sara sat up and stared toward the far cage, where he stood. He stormed away—and that's when Sara realized why he was upset.

The other woman had used her shirt and the bars to hang herself. The sleeves of her shirt were knotted together around her throat. Her body hung inches off the floor.

Sara closed her eyes for long seconds, filled with grief for the stranger. That poor woman had decided death was preferable to facing what might come.

Loud noises came closer, and she opened her eyes but avoided looking at the body.

The second guard returned with the first, both of them talking in high-pitched squeals. Their body language told Sara they were pissed. Both of them turned, glaring her way. She scooted to the far corner.

One stormed toward her, stopped outside her cage, and pressed the device at his throat.

"Give all clothing now!"

They didn't want to risk Sara ending her life, too.

She stood, shaking, and stripped.

Chapter One

The public hover transport engines came on and Sara's daily trip to a nearby city began. She lived in the alien city of Mors but had to work in Torq. It was a short ten-minute ride. She kept her bag with her lunch on her lap and her gaze down. Some aliens loved to stare at her...or worse.

The soft vibrations under her seat lulled her back to the recent past, to that day just one week ago since the transport had arrived on the planet Relon, where her buyer was supposed to pick her up.

She'd been so lucky.

Instead of her buyer, Relon's version of the police had stormed inside the shuttle when it landed. Turns out, slavery was illegal on their planet.

Law enforcement had freed her from her cell and arrested the guards. They'd assured her they would issue a warrant for the alien who'd purchased her, too, for daring to use Relon as a rendezvous. As far as Sara knew, he hadn't been caught so far.

The nice customs man who'd recorded all her information had explained that some planets were very remote, and her buyer was likely a resident of one of them. That's why the large port on Relon had become a hub of illegal trading. It was an ever-growing problem in recent months, and as a result, Relon police were checking all shuttles for illegal contraband.

That would include her.

Sara had refused to be sent back to Earth when they'd offered, too afraid her own government would just hand her back to the original aliens to be auctioned yet again. Instead, Relon's customs department had transferred her to a rescue shelter for freed slaves.

She had officially become a charity case.

The shelter provided her with a bed, three meals a day, a job, and clothing. They'd also given her a nifty red bracelet with a panic button in case anyone messed with her, ensuring the police would promptly respond. She'd gotten an implant inside her head, too. It translated the more than twenty alien languages that were spoken fluently on the planet.

However fortunate, Sara was slowly discovering there were just as many bad things about her new life on Relon.

The fifty-plus various alien females she lived with in the shelter hated humans, and gave her a wide berth. That made it impossible to make friends. It seemed a lot of people from Earth that far out in space were criminals or slavers. And it didn't bode well for Sara to be lumped in with them.

Indeed, the only two humans she'd met since coming to Relon had both been terrible. Men who'd tried to lure her into becoming a prostitute for them, claiming curiosity from alien men would earn them all a lot of credits. It made her sick to her stomach thinking about that kind of life.

The public hover transport shook, jolting Sara from her musings, and she glanced up. The alien male in a seat opposite her looked like a cross between a rabbit and lizard.

That could be one of her potential clients. *No way!*

She was currently headed to the job she'd been assigned. It was an easy one, serving drinks in a bar, and sometimes food in the dining area inside the same building. She sported some bruises on her ass from strange hands grabbing at her when she wasn't quick enough to avoid being fondled. Beggars couldn't be choosers, though. A job was required for her to get a bed and food. All her credits were saved, and in two months, the shelter would kick her out to fend for herself. That scared her, too.

"Yard, you're not paying attention to me!"

The shrill female voice startled her, and Sara turned her head, watching a white-haired blue alien in a tight dress punch the leg of a bigger blue alien man with jet-black hair. They appeared to be of the same race.

They looked somewhat human, only bigger boned, taller, and with that odd color. Their facial features were attractive—sharp cheekbones, full lips, and almost fully round eyes. The man had a super-muscular build, his black uniform stretched over a broad chest and thick biceps.

He grunted, taking the hard hit with barely a flinch.

"I apologize. My name is York." He had a deep voice.

The woman snorted and turned to a yellow alien female sitting next to her. That one was a bit shorter but rail thin and sporting four arms. "This is the best my father could do for me. Big and dumb, but he's got an excellent job. He works for an ambassador on one of those huge space vessels! You must train them right from the start. Remember that if you decide to bond with a Parri."

15

"I'm not going to," the thin alien replied, her voice cold. "I don't like submissive men."

"Why not? It's best to be in charge. Do you want one who'll bully you?" The blue woman shook her head. "Jazzatzz, you need to listen to me. Parri males *must* do the bidding of their bond mate. It's a matter of honor. This one will bow down to my every wish." She suddenly reached out and smacked the massive male again, this time on the arm. "Tell her, Yarv."

Sara flinched at the loud slap. It sounded painful.

The alien guy's lips only pressed together tightly before he responded. "We treat our bond mates extremely well. And my name is *York*."

The blue woman turned on him. "I don't like your tone! I'll call you what I want. The bonding ceremony doesn't take place until tomorrow morning; apologize, or I'll change my mind about becoming your mate. I'm doing you a great honor! Don't you ever forget that."

The big alien rolled his shoulders. "I apologize."

The woman smiled smugly, glancing at her friend. "See? You train them from the first moment you meet. We bare their children, sleep in their beds, and in return, we're to be treated with the highest respect. That's why you should choose to bond with a Parri. Other races are too barbaric."

Sara lowered her gaze, feeling sorry for York. The woman with him seemed to be a controlling bitch. She had been told some aliens mated, some bonded, and others signed legal contracts when they married. It had been covered in one of the classes the shelter provided every night. She'd also slowly been familiarizing herself with the different alien species living on Relon. She'd spotted some of the blue aliens before but had yet to get close enough to really study them or listen to them interact with each other.

"Yavor is buying me a new wardrobe before we fly off the surface to his job after the bonding ceremony. Only the best for me," the woman bragged. "That's one more reason you should pick a Parri, my friend. They aren't allowed to say no to their bond mates. He'll spoil me and give me whatever I want, or I'll make him suffer by refusing to allow him to cuddle me. Males need to hold their mates while they sleep."

Sara glanced back at York. He looked miserable as his fiancée or whatever she was rambled on about all the ways she could make the poor bastard suffer. Not once did she get his name right, blundering it every time.

Sara grew angry on his behalf.

The attractive man didn't correct the bitch after those first few times, but Sara noticed as his broad shoulders began to sag. Defeated had a look—and he wore it on his whole body. She knew it well, seeing it in her own expression every time she used a mirror as she got ready for work or before going to bed at the shelter.

He was going to be trapped with that bitch for life, just like she was stuck on Relon until she died.

The classes the shelter provided had said some aliens were basically set up by their families to marry. For others, it was about trade deals or making alliances. She wondered what York's story was. He couldn't have picked that blue bitch by choice. She was horrible to him.

The hover transport slowed and lowered, coming to a stop. Sara waited until the bigger aliens exited the craft before she got to her feet, not wanting to risk being trampled or groped. The blue couple walked ahead of her with the yellow alien at their side. They entered a store and she passed it. The blue alien woman smacked the big guy yet again, that time on the chest, but she couldn't hear the words.

"Poor bastard," Sara whispered.

A block down, she reached the bar and walked around to the side entrance. A big green alien with horns nodded at her and opened the door. She entered, put her lunch bag inside the cubby her boss had assigned her, and then tied on an apron. Minutes later, she was serving drinks.

Time passed fast, since there were a lot of customers. She dodged groping hands and tentacles. That still took some practice; a few of the aliens had six arms. One guy even sported pinchers. She avoided him entirely, fearing he'd take off body parts with those sharp appendages.

Her boss finally let her know when it was time for a break and she fled into the back to retrieve her lunch. The room she ate in was tiny but at least it gave her privacy. She finished and used the bathroom, washed her hands, and returned to work. Her boss jerked one of his two thumbs toward the dining area, and she was grateful to go. Most of the customers who came in for food weren't drunk or grabby.

The other waitress caught her up on orders, which tables were waiting for food, and who had just entered. Sara took the electronic pad and walked to a table. "Welcome to Vay. Are you ready to order?"

18

The red-skinned devil-looking alien stared her up and down. "What are you?"

She really hated that question, seeming to answer it a hundred times a day. Her boss had ordered her to always be polite to the customers. "A human from Earth."

He sniffed at her. "You smell like food."

She took a step back, praying he didn't try to take a bite out of her. "I'm not. I only serve it. Check out the menu. That's what's available."

"Do you bleed red?"

That scared her even more. "I'll give you more time to decide." She turned and attempted to flee, slamming into a hard body.

"I'm so very sorry." She looked up—and gasped. It was the blue guy from the hover transport.

"Did I hurt you? You're quite a tiny human."

He was a good foot taller than her, probably six-six or seven. Huge up close, and even more brawny than she'd thought; easy to tell, since she'd just slammed into him. His body was hard-packed with muscle. There was a blue insignia on his black uniform, probably the name of the ship he worked on.

And he knew what she was. That came as a surprise. Most aliens had to ask.

She peered up at his face. "I'm actually not tiny. I'm average-sized for a woman...well, from my planet. I'm so sorry I bumped into you. It's my fault."

"I'm big and difficult to avoid in small quarters." He gave her a dazzling smile. "You couldn't damage me if you tried. Are you sure I didn't hurt you? I know humans bruise easily."

That offhanded remark alarmed her, and it must have shown on her face.

The blue skin darkened on his face. "Not that I would ever hurt one. A few of my crew are bonded to female humans."

That surprised her again, but she tried to keep her expression neutral. Bonded meant married. And so far, she'd been pretty sure women from Earth were only bought and sold by aliens to be sexual slaves. "I'm fine. Do you need me to show you and your party to a table?"

"It's just me, and yes, I need a table."

She turned, glanced around, and found an empty one in the corner. She led him there and pushed a button on her pad. A menu hologram appeared above the table. "Have a seat. I'll give you a few minutes."

He sat his big frame in the chair. "Thank you."

She wondered where the two alien women had gone as she returned to the devil alien. He sniffed at her and made her uncomfortable again when he ordered raw meat. He was one of *those*. The fresher the kill, the better. There was a squid alien who came in sometimes who ate his food still squirming. His favored dish was live fish in a bowl.

She picked up a tray to serve another table and then returned to York.

"Have you decided what you want to eat?"

"I'll have the Parri plate. It's the only thing from my old planet that you serve."

She tapped the screen, sending his order to the kitchen. "To drink?"

"Hoser."

That was the equivalent of beer on Relon. She tapped it into the pad. "It should be five minutes for your meal but I'll get your drink from the bar now."

She began to turn away when he gently brushed her arm with his fingers. She startled slightly, then faced him.

"Sorry. I don't know your name. I didn't mean offense by touching you. Can I ask you something?"

"Sure."

"What are you doing on Relon?"

"I was taken from my planet and sold." She hesitated. "The Relon police found me before I was handed over to the buyer."

"I thought this planet was good about sending victims back to their home worlds?"

"They offered. I decided not to return."

She didn't want to explain that Earth officials had been responsible in the first place. It would probably only make the bad reputation of humans even worse.

She fled, getting his beer and picking up food for the devil alien. He sat at his table sipping something that looked like blood. A shudder ran down her spine as she placed his raw meat in front of him. The way he looked at her left little doubt that he'd prefer to eat *her*.

21

Another group of customers came in. She got them a table and found out what they wanted, then she picked up York's order, taking it to him. As she approached, she noticed he looked depressed, maybe sad, until she put the plate in front of him. His food appeared to be cooked meat with some kind of rice.

He smiled. "Thank you."

"You're welcome. Enjoy. Wave at me if you need something before you finish."

"You could tell me your name."

She met his eyes. They were beautiful. A dark blue framed by long black eyelashes. "Sara."

"Thank you, Sara."

She turned away, glancing around the room. The dining area was small, only ten tables. All the customers had food. She spun back around. "May I ask *you* something, York?"

His head snapped up and he stared at her. "How did you know my name?"

She felt her cheeks warm. "Um, we were on that hover transport from the city together."

"We were?" He frowned. "I didn't see you."

"I was seated in the corner. You were sitting near me. I kind of overheard some things."

"Oh." His face darkened again. She hoped it wasn't anger that made his pale blue skin turn that color.

"Forget I said anything. I'm sorry. Enjoy your meal." She started to flee but he reached out, lightly grasping her arm. She met his gaze.

"What did you want to know?"

"It's none of my business, but…you seem like a nice person." *Alien. Whatever.* "Your woman…*isn't*. Are you being forced to marry her?"

He released his gentle grip on her arm. "No."

That confused her more. "Then why? She's kind of…" She paused, not wanting to insult him.

He glanced at her and his face darkened again.

"My apologies. Humans are curious. Please forget I said anything."

"No. It's fine." He sighed. "Two of my crew have bonded with females. They seem so happy, and… It makes me lonely. There are a lot of single females on Relon. I went to one of those places that find ones who want bond mates, and they eventually paired me with Nodo."

"Oh."

"I frightened the other women. It's my size. They think I'm dangerous and violent. Nodo was the only one interested in bonding to me."

Sara frowned. "The woman was smacking and punching you. And you just took it. Anyone with violent tendencies would have knocked her on her ass." She paused. "I would have."

He grinned. "You're funny."

"I'm serious. I hate being hit."

All humor fled from his face. "Who hits you? Do you need help? Point them out to me and I'll make sure they don't do it again. I'd never hit a female, but I would pulverize a male. There's no excuse to abuse someone as delicate as you."

Her heart missed a beat. He looked sincerely outraged, and she'd never been called "delicate" before. Stout. Big boned. Pudgy more times than she could count. Never delicate. Sara found she liked it. "It was while I was on Earth. Thank you, though. The shelter people take good care of me. They gave me this job."

One of her customers caught her attention by waving a tentacle. "I have to go."

She fled to get a drink refill and serve other tables...but her gaze kept returning to York. He used some kind of data-communications pad while he ate. When he finally finished, she walked over to him.

"May I get you anything else?"

"I'm good. I must pick up Nodo and her best friend. They're probably done eating by now."

"Why didn't you eat with them?"

Misery flashed in his eyes. "She didn't want me to."

That revelation filled her with sympathy for York. She held out her tablet, and he pressed his thumb to it to transfer credits to pay his bill. He stood, and Sara lifted her chin high; he really was tall. He began to walk around her, but she reached out to touch *his* arm that time.

He stilled, looking down at her.

"There's this saying on Earth. Run, don't walk to the nearest exit."

"I don't understand. I'm leaving."

"I meant from Nodo. She's horrible. You could do much better. *Much*," she emphasized. "I would return to your ship and fly away without her. You might be lonely, but that's better than being with someone who makes you unhappy. That woman is pure misery."

He sighed. "I have no choice."

"You said you aren't being forced into it."

"She's the only one willing to leave the surface and bond with me. My two best friends have females, and now spend all their free time with them. The rest of the crew keeps to themselves. My kind doesn't do well with silence for long stretches. I need companionship. I've been suffering depression, and it's growing worse. I need a bond mate. At least Nodo will talk to me."

"She doesn't even care enough to remember your name, York. And I heard you say it more than once. You're a handsome guy. Big, sure, but you seem super nice. You deserve better. Please don't settle. That's another Earth saying. You'll find someone who won't treat you so badly."

"You don't understand..."

Maybe she didn't. He looked unhappy but determined. She knew it wasn't worth arguing with him. It was *his* life. There was a lot more to learn about aliens than the little she had gleaned in a week.

She released him and backed away, giving him one last imploring look before moving to another table.

York left but Sara kept thinking about him during the hours that passed until her shift ended. She clocked out, walking back toward the transport that would return her near the shelter.

25

Aliens stared at her, and Sara tucked her head down. A few of them called out to ask what she was. She just kept moving.

"Sara!"

The booming deep voice had her spinning, and she spotted York moving through the crowd, his height making him taller than everyone around him. She waited for him, surprised, and gazed around, looking for Nodo while wondering why York wanted to talk to her.

He stopped in front of her. "Let me escort you home."

"Where's Nodo?"

"She wanted to spend her last night on Relon with her best friend. I won't see her again until tomorrow morning at the records department."

"Well...I live in Mors."

"That's where I'm staying, too, and will be bonded there in the morning. Please, let me escort you."

"Pretty."

The creepy voice had Sara turning her head to stare up at one of those rabbit-looking lizard aliens. He'd snuck up on her, his beady gaze locked on her breasts.

"Move on, Yuna," York snarled, his voice turning harsh. "The female isn't interested."

The alien sniffed long and loud. "Not yours." He reached into his pocket and pulled out a credit bar. "Come with me and I pay to touch you."

She sighed, beyond irritated with those kinds of offers. "I'm not a sex worker."

"Go away." York gently cupped her elbow and pulled her closer to his body, glaring at the smaller alien. Then he curled his upper lip, flashing two vampire-like fangs.

The Yuna hissed and backed off before fleeing.

York frowned and looked down at her. "Do you get that often?"

"Every day, at least a dozen times. I've been told I'm a curiosity." She lifted her wrist, showing the red bracelet. "Most of them flee when I make it clear I'm not interested and flash this. In an emergency, I can press these two buttons together. It's a personal alarm from the shelter. The police are supposed to rush to me."

"I've seen a few of those but never knew what they were for."

She let her hand drop. "Women freed from slavers get them while we're under the protection of the shelter. It's to prevent us from being snatched and sold."

"Now I *insist* on escorting you home." He glared at the aliens around them. "To make sure no one else bothers you."

"You don't have to do that."

He smiled. "I want to. There aren't a lot of humans this far out in space. I like the ones who bonded to my crew members."

"Were they rescued from slavers, too?"

"I'll tell you on the hover transport."

"I'd like that."

Chapter Two

Sara grinned. "Nara actually did that?"

York nodded, a smile curving his lips. "She fell in love with Cathian and wasn't about to lose him."

"Is he like you?"

York chuckled. "You mean a Parri? No. Cathian is a Tryleskian. We're about the same size though."

The information surprised her. "And they...*work*?"

York lowered his voice. "Yes, if you're talking about sex. They want to have a litter with his next heat."

A litter? Heat? As in, going into heat? She was bemused by those terms, but she guessed a Tryleskian had to be some type of animal alien.

"The scientists they consulted are certain it will happen. They are biologically compatible to have young."

"It's great that they can have kids. I mean, you know, being from different planets."

He nodded. "It's the theory of the Seeders."

"What's that?"

"Some scholars on various planets believe there used to be an ancient alien race that left life on each planet. They were great-distance travelers, and they might explain why some of our genetics are somewhat compatible. The scholars believe that, long ago, we were all the same race. But life on each planet, depending on its conditions, mutated over time."

She glanced around the hover transport and spotted a pink alien who resembled a large sponge. It didn't have arms or legs. "That's difficult to believe."

He followed her gaze and chuckled. "You and I are not compatible with the Yo. Few races are."

"I really need to learn more about aliens."

"How long have you been on Relon?"

"Only a week. This is the first alien world I've ever visited, and now I live here."

"It must be overwhelming."

"You have no idea. I'm scared all the time. Everything is so vastly different here than on Earth."

"Why don't you return to your planet, Sara?"

"That's an embarrassing question."

"You saw *me* with Nodo..."

She nodded, acknowledging his point. "I'm considered very poor on Earth, and there are way more women than men on my planet. That seems to make us commodities in the minds of some jerks. They sold me to aliens."

"Who did?"

"Earth. As in, the government made a deal with aliens, and the military handed us over to them. I didn't volunteer for this. They forced me. Women-for-technology kind of trade deal. It's why I can't risk going back. They'd probably just arrest me and shove me onto another transport off world. Next time, customs might not find and rescue me.

And some alien with a harem of women had bought me to be a sex slave. No thanks."

He looked angry. "Some planets frequently sell their own people for gain. I'm sorry it happened to you, Sara."

"Me too."

"You must miss your family very much."

"I didn't have any. It was only me and my mom. She passed away two years ago."

He reached out as if to take her hand, but then stopped. "What about your father?"

"My mom got around."

"She traveled?"

Sara smiled. York had no clue what she meant. It was rather charming. "She slept with a lot of men. When she got pregnant, she wasn't sure who my father was."

"She wasn't bonded to a male?"

"No. She never married."

"My race can have sex with others, but not create children until after a couple has bonded. Once we do, it changes the chemicals in our bodies, to make us fertile. After the bond, I'll only want that one female."

She let that information settle in...and liked what she heard. Her mother hadn't meant to get pregnant with Sara. It had been rough growing up without a dad and being taunted by others for it. That wouldn't happen with a Parri, if only bonded pairs had kids. The idea of a couple only wanting the person they'd bonded with sounded nice, too.

She'd heard some races mated for life, never cheating or straying on each other.

"Sara? You've gone silent. Have I said something to upset you?"

She met York's beautiful gaze. "No. I'm always learning something new here."

He grinned. "Cathian, my captain and best friend, can only get his life-lock pregnant while in heat every three years."

She pondered that. "Does that mean they only have sex when he's in heat?"

He chuckled. "They have sex often." His humor faded. "It's why I'm always alone. The Pods keep to themselves. Midgel, our cook, spends all her time alone, too. Dovis, my other best friend, just found his mate. They lock themselves in their cabin to have sex when they aren't working. Raff is single, but he doesn't like to talk. And Marrow is spending all her free time searching for her own mate, contacting other planets on our comms to talk to different males."

"They're the rest of the crew on your ship?"

He nodded as a look of misery crossed his face again. "I am hoping that once Nodo and I are alone, she won't be so distant. It was rough on all Parri when our planet began to die. Some of us accepted our new circumstances but others are still bitter. Time should help her heal. I'll help her as well. Mass evacuations took place just over three years ago. It's difficult, knowing you are without a world and dependent upon others to share theirs."

"I'm so sorry." The idea disturbed her.

He nodded. "My people lost everything. I was lucky to find a job with Captain Cathian on *The Vorge*. Nodo and her family ended up here. There's a Parri settlement, but they aren't happy living on Relon. They were given an old section of town to call their own. Her family used to be wealthy, but now they're considered indigent. She wants to live in comfort again."

"She was terrible to you. You deserve better, York. I still think you should wait to find someone else."

He sighed, staring into her eyes. "I'm suffering depression all the time. Parri are social by nature. My friends kept me from feeling loneliness but now they have their females to occupy their free time. I need a mate, too. The choices are few for my kind. The Parri have been shoved into overpopulated settlements on various planets or become homeless wanderers." He gave a sad smile. "Refugees aren't exactly on any female's wish list as an ideal male. I live on a vessel. I was fortunate that Nodo even agreed to be my bond mate."

Sara let the topic drop. He looked miserable enough without her pointing out yet again what a bitch Nodo was. Maybe the alien woman would be nicer once she didn't have her friend around. Sara highly doubted it, though.

The hover transport slowed and lowered, coming to a stop. The doors opened and the other passengers exited. She glanced around, seeing familiar buildings. The trip was over.

"This is my stop."

York got up and offered his hand. "Mine, too. I'll walk you to your home to make certain you get there safely."

She reached up and clasped his hand. It felt good in hers, comforting and warm. "Thank you. The shelter is close."

They walked side by side down the street. He kept hold of her hand and slowed his pace to a stop in front of the building she'd indicated was her destination.

"Sara?"

She looked up him. "Yes?"

He paused, glancing around, seeming almost nervous before looking back down at her. Finally, he said, "Thank you for talking to me. I've enjoyed our conversation."

"Me too. Thank you for escorting me home."

"I wish you luck on Relon. Are you going to be searching for a mate?"

She shook her head. "I don't think so. Not for a while, anyway. I've got a lot to learn before I make any life-altering decisions."

He gave a nod, glancing away again. "I will wait until you go inside before going to my lodgings. I wish we could talk longer. The bonding ceremony isn't until nine in the morning, but I need to pack my belongings. Once the ceremony is over, Nodo wants me to take her shopping, and then a shuttle will fly us up to *The Vorge*." His gaze returned to hers, his expression almost...wistful. "Be safe and well, Sara."

"You too. Good luck, York."

She turned away reluctantly and left him in front of the building. He was the closest thing to a friend she'd made since reaching Relon, and he was leaving the planet in the morning.

Bonding to a bitch.

33

She shook her head, waved her wristband at the lock on the door, and it slid open. She turned back for one last look at York. He watched her silently. Sara lifted her hand in a final wave before entering.

Inside, various alien women were talking amongst themselves. Most of them ignored her or shot her distrustful looks. She went to her bunk in the sleeping section of the building and rested, waiting for dinner. When the bell finally rang, she followed everyone to the dining hall, getting in line. A few of the women whispered, gossiping about her just loud enough for her to overhear the insults.

"I'm not some plant sent here to pick out targets to be kidnapped," she loudly declared to one of them, getting fed up. "I was *sold* by my own kind. Understand?"

"Humans are vile beings," the woman hissed, flashing a row of sharp teeth. She reminded Sara of a shark with limbs. "Untrustworthy slavers!"

Sara was already beginning to hate her new life. The women didn't trust her and the men kept offering her money to sleep with them. Was that her future? What she'd have to deal with year in and year out?

It finally became her turn, and she got her plate of food then carried it to a table. No one sat with her. They grouped together, staying away. She lowered her head, eating quietly.

York kept entering her mind. He had the kindest eyes she'd ever seen. He also seemed to be a really good person, and so desperate to no longer be alone. His refugee status wasn't a problem as far as Sara was concerned. She didn't have a home world anymore, either. Earth had betrayed her, and there was no going back. That still stung, and she knew it would for a long time.

34

Tomorrow morning, he'd bond to Nodo the bitch, get treated like crap, and end up miserable. It wasn't fair that such a nice guy had that kind of future awaiting him. Then again, she didn't deserve her rotten fate, either. She'd been a good person all her life. Never stealing or treating others badly.

Nice people got screwed in the end, she decided.

Tears filled her eyes but she blinked them back. Self-pity wasn't going to do a thing but make her eyes puffy and give her a runny nose. She finished her meal and went to the classroom in the basement of the building.

Two instructors waited. Tonight, they taught the women about various neighborhoods on Relon, and which ones would be safest for them to move into when they got their own apartments. When the class ended, Sara approached one of the Relon males.

He looked at her with a smile. "You have questions?"

"Yes. What can you tell me about a Parri?"

He cocked his head. "Did you visit their settlement?"

"No, but I met one. He's getting bonded. I was curious about that."

He studied her. "Why?"

"Is it possible for a Parri to bond with a human?" The question burst out of her unexpectantly, but she didn't regret asking.

He glanced down at the pad in his hand, tapping it. "There have been two records of Parri and human bonding filed in the last three years. Neither has been revoked." He looked up at her. "I would assume it's possible."

"What does bonding to a Parri require?"

He looked down at his pad, tapping it once more. He read from the screen, "Fluid exchanges during sexual encounters with the pair." He turned the pad her way.

Sara gaped. It was a picture of a naked Parri male, his face blurred out, but she got a full-frontal view. Their bodies looked human, except bigger, and were that same light blue—every inch of them. The male in the picture was aroused, and she couldn't help but feel a tinge of trepidation. That was the biggest cock she'd ever seen. It looked long and thick.

She lifted her gaze to find the Relon grinning.

"Most females who consider a Parri change their minds after seeing one nude. Their average height is seven feet tall, and they are the largest race body-wise who live on Relon."

He turned his pad and tapped again, then showed her another image. It was a photo of a naked human man, his face blurred out, too. There were markings on the wall behind him. She could tell this guy was much shorter than York, a bit on the thin side, and his cock looked small in comparison when he was aroused.

"Do you want to see the side-by-side comparison?"

She shook her head, looking up at him. "No thank you."

"I wouldn't suggest spending time with their males. A bonded Parri male needs skin-to-skin contact with a female often. They have a difficult time feeling happy, sleeping, or maintaining an appetite without constant physical interaction, once the bond is formed. That means regular sexual and skin contact. Your race is frailer than theirs. Though, the males *are*

36

extremely mellow unless they're in protective mode." He tapped on his screen, and then showed her yet another picture.

She felt her dinner almost come up and raised a hand, covering her mouth. It was an image of one of those rabbit-looking lizard aliens, only he was in pieces. Something had torn his limbs off and crushed in part of his head.

She now knew that particular race had green blood.

The Relon blanked the screen and folded the pad against his chest. "That is what a Parri male did to a Yuna for touching his bond mate. The Yuna did not survive. Security reached them in under a minute, but damage is done quickly when the male Parri is in protective mode. There have been no reports of them harming females, but you *would* be subjected to a demonstration of their extreme ability to commit violence if you were ever assaulted by another male." He touched the device and turned it once more. "I would choose the Avials, if blue males are your preference."

She stared at the screen. It was another nude blue alien, this one with a slim body. His face was blurred but he had long braided hair that fell almost to his waist. His penis was thin and would be considered average, if he were human.

The Relon explained, "They are a peaceful race who have a settlement here as well. The Avials grow herbs and other plants, never eating the flesh of animals. They have no violent tendencies."

"Can you tell me more about the Parri?"

He looked disapproving. "Avials are a better selection for you, if you wish to marry someone from another race. Parri males are too large." His glanced down at her body. "You're a fragile species."

She'd heard him the first time. "Thank you for the information." She didn't want to start an argument or upset him. The instructors were her only source of information on her new planet. "I'll think about it."

She had just a few more questions. "Where exactly do the bonding ceremonies take place in Mar?"

"The records department."

"How many are there?"

"One in each city."

"And what do bonding ceremonies entail?"

"Blood samples to make sure your races are compatible, an agreement not to do each other harm or hold our planet responsible for anything and, depending on the race, there can be a fluid exchange."

"Like a kiss?"

He nodded. "Mouth-to-mouth touching is common with many races."

"Got it. Thank you." She walked away, returning upstairs to her bunk. The other women were already getting ready for bed, some having earlier work shifts than Sara. None of them spoke to her, of course. Humans just weren't popular on Relon; she'd have to get used to that treatment if she stayed there.

She lay down, staring at the bunk over hers, thinking about York. He seemed super nice, and that Parri woman was truly awful...maybe Sara could offer to be his mate?

The sex sounded a bit scary though. He was huge, and now she had no doubt his cock would be, too, if he looked anything like that picture she'd seen. She thought she could deal with cuddling him skin to skin. York had been gentle every time he'd touched her.

Sara tried to rest but sleep wouldn't come. She thought about her old life on Earth. She'd lived in a tiny apartment, her mother her only family. Her death had been extremely hard on Sara. She'd had some friends, though, who had gotten her through her grief.

They were probably worried about her, since she hadn't been allowed to tell anyone goodbye or that she was being sent off world. Now she was completely alone on Relon. Making friends on her new home world wasn't going to be an option, unless someone overlooked where she came from.

Chapter Three

Sara woke earlier than normal thanks to a few of the women getting into an argument. Someone's shoes had gone missing. An orange fish-looking woman smacked around a mouse-like female, who made screeching noises until other women broke them apart. That was a common occurrence, living in the shelter. Different kinds of aliens put together from various worlds tended to argue quite a bit, sometimes getting into physical altercations.

She went into the bathroom and took a shower. A bird-like woman hissed at her as she got out. "Slaver." She spat on the floor at her feet.

Sara sighed. "I am *not* a slaver." That was getting old fast. "I was taken from my planet and sold. I'm just like you."

"Lies!" the alien hissed, stepping closer.

The woman suddenly threw a punch.

Sara had grown up in rough neighborhoods; fighting was nothing new. She dodged the strike, nearly slipping on the damp floor, then swiftly threw her towel over the woman's head. She gave her a hard shove into one of the shower stalls being used by someone else. The women instantly began to screech at each other and fight.

Sara hurried away, relieved when she wasn't followed and attacked. She went to her bunk and took clean clothing out of the drawer under her bed. It didn't take long to get dressed. When she entered the dining area, she noticed a lot of women glowering at her. Again.

She stopped, meeting their gazes one by one.

"Not all humans are slavers. I was sold by my own kind. How many times do I have to say it? What is *wrong* with all of you? We should stick together, not pick on each other."

They just continued giving her dirty looks.

She sighed and made it to the front of the line, picking up a bowl of what passed for oatmeal and a glass of some veggie drink popular on Relon. No one sat with her as she ate, as usual, and her gaze kept going to the clock. She'd have to leave at half past nine to be on time for work. One hour.

The woman from the shower came in with two others who appeared to be from the same race. They headed straight toward Sara.

She stood, prepared for the worst, dread filling her. She was outnumbered, and they looked angry enough to do some damage.

Right at that moment, one of the guards walked in to get a drink.

The women glanced at him before quickly changing direction.

They were still going to attack her when given the chance. New planet, same old crap. Bullies existed everywhere. Only now, she wasn't being targeted for not having a father or being poorer than most, but for being born human.

She fled the dining area to go back to her bunk. York flashed in her mind yet again. She pushed thoughts of him back and decided it was best to leave for work early.

She left the building and headed toward the hover transport, men staring at her. A few blocked her path, offering her credits to allow them to touch her. One even tried to grope her breast. She slapped his tentacle away.

The transport loomed, and she quickly reached it...but hesitated at the door.

One of the men already inside smiled, giving her body leering glances. "What are you?"

The way he visually inspected her body made her skin crawl. "Fed up."

"I haven't heard of that race. Which planet are you from? I'll pay you if you let me take you home. Your skin looks soft and delectable." His tongue flicked out, revealing it was forked. Next, he made soft moaning noises.

Why did aliens always assume she might say yes? It was never going to happen.

"I can't do this every day of my life," she muttered, mostly to herself. "I just can't. I'm a person with *feelings*. Not a sex toy, damn it! I didn't end up on this planet to be propositioned by idiots all the time!"

He looked surprised, mouth hanging open.

She spun around and stormed to one of the visitor information booths next to the transportation station. "Tell me where the records department is, please."

The automated system showed her a map with symbols, and the image of one particular building glowed on the screen. She memorized the location, since she couldn't read the Relon language. It was only about four blocks away. She turned left and sprinted in that direction.

What if she were too late? What if York and the bitch had gotten there early and their alien version of marriage was a done deal?

Panic set in as she ran faster.

She found the building with a group of people waiting outside. It appeared the offices hadn't opened for business yet. Sara spotted York easily, standing taller than the rest of the people there. She grinned, heading right toward him.

She had to wiggle between bodies to reach him. He was near the front of the group, closest to the door. Nodo was with him, as well as her yellow-skinned friend. Sara came to a stop behind York, tried to catch her breath, and then gently tapped on his broad back.

He turned, staring down at her. Surprise widened his eyes. "What are you doing here, Sara?"

"Yeppel, I was talking to you!" Nodo stepped around him, spotted Sara, and growled low in her throat.

Sara faced her. "His name is *York*." She sounded it out for the blue bitch—twice. "It's not hard to say. You could at least try to be polite enough to make the effort to learn it." Her gaze locked with his. "Don't bond to her, York. It will be a mistake."

Nodo gasped loudly. "Get away from my bond mate!"

Sara ignored her, peering into York's beautiful blue eyes. "You said some of your crew were bonded to humans. I know we don't know each other well but I promise I'll be nice to you. I won't be anything like *her*." She waved her hand at Nodo. "Pick *me* instead. *I'll* be your mate."

Nodo snarled. "This pathetic alien is attempting to lure my future bond mate away. Call a guard!" She screeched louder. "Guard!"

York appeared stunned for a heartbeat or two but recovered quickly—and smiled. "I wanted to ask you yesterday when I walked you home, but you said you weren't looking for a mate. What changed your mind?"

Sara began to tell him but Nodo's friend stepped closer, drawing her attention.

"Ugly alien! Scat!" The yellow woman tried to shoo Sara away, waving her hands as if she didn't want to touch her.

Sara shot her a scowl before staring back at York. "You're lonely. I'm all alone, too. And neither one of us wants to be unhappy. We can make it work—together," Sara said quickly. The strangers around them had backed off, and Nodo was screeching for a guard again. "I'll bond with you, York. Please say yes!"

Loud footsteps sounded, and Sara turned her head, fear lancing through her as two Relons in police-type uniforms rushed toward them. One of the males reached out to grab her arm, but York suddenly lunged, stepping in front of her.

"Leave the human alone. She's going to be my bond mate." York's voice came out deep and clear.

"What?" Nodo gasped.

York turned, gently placed his hand on Sara's lower back, and pulled her closer to his body. "I don't want to bond with you, Nagway."

Sara grinned. She couldn't see around his bulky body but she heard the screech coming from his other side.

"That's not my name!" The blue bitch sounded outraged.

"Now you know how it feels." York stepped away from her, pulling Sara with him. "I revoke my offer to bond with you."

"You promised to buy me clothes, to take me off this horrible planet! You're going to give me a better life!"

"And I thought you'd be nice. You're not." York turned, keeping Sara against him, and met her gaze. "Let's do this." He smiled again.

Sara grinned back. "Let's."

"Yard!" Nodo yelled.

He turned his attention to the police. "You should take her away. I don't want some outraged Parri female scaring my timid human."

Sara didn't correct him. Maybe it was best he thought of her that way until after they were bonded.

She watched as the police herded an angry and outraged pair of females away from the building. Nodo yelled threats at York, promising she'd tell her father about what he'd done and make him pay. She even screamed about getting him fired from his job.

That last threat worried Sara. "Can she do that? Get you fired?" She didn't want him to suffer in any way.

York shook his head. "No. What *really* made you decide to bond to me, Sara?"

Another loud screech came from Nodo down the street. "He said he'd buy me new clothes! I want my clothes! Do you hear me, Yavor? You owe me an expensive wardrobe!"

Sara bit back a laugh, not feeling one ounce of pity for Nodo. "I had to save you from *that*. Isn't that reason enough?"

He chuckled. "Yes. And I'm grateful."

"You don't even have to buy me clothes," she boasted with a grin. "I have a few other sets where I live. We could swing by the shelter to pick them up."

"Do you like them?"

Sara shrugged. "They were assigned to me."

"Do you have any personal belongings at the shelter that matter?"

"No. I left Earth with the clothes I had on that day. They wouldn't allow us to get any of our possessions."

He held out his hand to her. "Then I'll buy you clothes. It will be a privilege. Parri enjoy spoiling their females."

"I'm not like *her*, York. You don't need to do that."

"You need clothing, Sara. Allow me to provide for you as your bond mate."

He really was as nice as she'd thought. She gripped his big hand and relaxed for the first time since leaving Earth. Maybe it wouldn't be a huge mistake after all to marry an alien.

The doors opened at nine and York led her inside the records department. It took some time to find the right office for bonding

46

ceremonies, and the robed Relon male scowled when he saw the bracelet on her wrist.

"What is this? She's under the protection of the shelter for freed slaves."

Sara released York's hand and tapped in the code she'd been given when the bracelet had been put on, taking it off. "Not anymore." She placed it on the desk. "I want to bond with York."

The Relon leaned in closely to peer at her face. "I detect no fear or stress. This is your free will? The male isn't threatening you?"

"No. I mean yes. No, he isn't threatening me. Yes, I want to do this."

"Understood." The Relon took out a pad and held it toward them. "Place your hand on here."

York went first. The Relon read off the pad after York pulled his hand away. "One hundred percent Parri. You work for the Tryleskian ambassador. Your last health scan was only a few days ago when you applied to find a bond mate through the matching agency." He paused, glanced at Sara, and then eyed York. "This is not the Parri female who chose you."

"Sara is better."

The Relon looked at Sara, holding out the pad. "I see. Your turn. The male is healthy, has never bonded before, and is free to join with you. No arrest warrants or criminal history."

She was impressed with the information the Relon clerk shared with her. They sure didn't give any information about grooms on Earth. She placed her palm on the pad.

47

He pulled it back, reading what it had returned on her. "Rescued from a slaver transport. Born on Earth. One hundred percent human. Medical cleared her as heathy and gave her all updated vaccines and a translation implant." He glanced at York. "No previous life records of any kind are available from her home planet. The medical scans taken have shown she has all reproductive organs in place." He stood. "Let's find out if she's compatible. Blood samples now."

It was both odd and impersonal when each of them were jabbed in the finger with some alien needle attached to yet another pad, but the Relon deemed them compatible. She had questions about what exactly that meant, but he shoved still another pad at them, asking for their handprints after extracting promises that they swore not to maim or kill each other. York had to swear not to sell her, possibly because of how she'd ended up on the planet. They each pressed their hands to the pad and the Relon retook his seat.

"Your bonding is recorded. Take her to exchange fluids to seal the bond. You have three days to contact records if you wish to nullify." He hit a button. "Next!"

Sara was dazed. That was it?

York led her out as another alien couple entered the room. They didn't speak until they were back on the street. York stopped, peering at her. "Are you feeling regret?"

"No. That wasn't what I was expecting. I'm just a little stunned over how fast it happened. I thought it would take longer. That's not a bad thing, though."

"How do humans record their bonding?"

"It doesn't matter. We're not on Earth. When the clerk said we're compatible after talking about my reproductive organs, does that mean we can have children together?"

He nodded. "Yes."

That revelation left her feeling uncertain. He was a *big* alien. She wasn't sure she'd survive if she ever got pregnant. Parri babies were probably larger than a human one would be.

York bent forward a little, catching her attention. "It will work out between us. I would never hurt you in any way, Sara. Are you worried about sealing our bond?"

"Sex, right? He said exchange fluids."

"I won't rush you, and when you are reacy, I will be very gentle."

That was a relief, at least. "Thank you."

"Thank *you*, Sara. You saved me from Nodo. I think my crew would have hated her." He suddenly grinned. "But they will love *you*. I'm bringing home another human." A deep, rumbling chuckle came from him. "Dovis and Cathian will be surprised."

"Your best friends, right?"

"Yes. Let me take you shopping. Are you hungry?"

"I ate breakfast already." And she almost felt like throwing up. The reality of what she'd done began to sink in.

She'd married a big blue alien. Her life had changed drastically in the two weeks since she'd been taken from her workplace.

* * * * *

49

York was worried. Sara hadn't spoken much since they'd left the bonding ceremony. Unlike Nodo, she also wasn't demanding. She acted shy and seemed hesitant to allow him to buy her outfits. He helped her pick each item, assuring her she'd need many. He kept reminding himself that Relon was the first planet she'd visited after leaving the one she'd lived on since birth. It must be frightening for her. He needed to be extra sensitive to her needs.

"Are you well, Sara? I'm concerned."

She gazed up at him. He found her extremely attractive. She had light brown hair that fell to her shoulders, and big green eyes. Her figure was pleasantly rounded. He guessed she was inches taller than Nara and Mari, and he liked her delicate features. She had pale skin, generous lips, and her voice was pleasant to listen to. Her hips were wide, too, which boded well for breeding and being with a male of his size. He wasn't worried about accidently harming her when they did complete their bonding.

"Yes." She placed her hand on his arm. "It's just nerves, and I'm worried about the money you're spending on me. I don't want you going into debt over me. That's no way to start a marriage. You don't need to impress me, York."

He relaxed. "I make good credits working for the Tryleskians. We will live on *The Vorge*. That means you'll need clothing and other things, since we travel all the time, and often don't stop for weeks. The replicators on *The Vorge* are good, but they don't have many choices like the stores on the planets and stations offer. Allow me to spoil you. You're my bonded female. I want to take care of you, Sara."

50

She smiled, the tension in her face easing. "Just don't overdo it by spending too much. I wasn't raised with a lot of possessions. I don't need much. I have no idea how money works off Earth. We had classes every night at the shelter but I have a lot to learn. Everything is still so new to me."

"I'm going to take care of you." He felt his chest swell with pride. Sara needed him. And unlike Nodo, she cared enough to be considerate. "Are you hungry? Be honest with me."

"No. Did you eat? We could stop somewhere if you haven't." Her smile widened. "I'd be honored to sit with you."

"I ate."

"Then we're good."

The merchant packed a few bags with the clothing York had purchased and he accepted them. He offered Sara his arm and led her to another store that sold female products he thought she might enjoy. He had to tell her what things were, and she picked a few scented washes for her hair and body.

Before long, they headed toward the shuttle port, where they'd catch a ride off the planet and go to *The Vorge*. He couldn't wait to introduce her to the crew.

He was grateful he'd cleaned his cabin before coming down to the surface, since he'd planned to find a female to bond with. It would have been a bad start to their relationship if Sara knew he tended to be messy. It hadn't mattered when he'd lived alone. There had been no one to impress. Now things were different.

He still felt a little stunned that Sara had found him and offered to be his bond mate. The grin on his face wouldn't go away. She was much nicer than Nodo. Now, instead of being worried about how his crew would react, he felt excitement. Nara and Mari would love Sara as much as he was already beginning to.

The transport shuttles came into view—but York abruptly halted, spotting a small group of Parri waiting. He identified one of the angry-looking males immediately.

A grumble of irritation escaped his lips.

"What's wrong?" Sara pressed her body against his side, and then she softly cursed. "Shit. I see the problem. Is that Nodo's dad, and maybe her two brothers?"

"I don't know who the other males are, but yes, that's her father. Nodo has no brothers. They are probably males from the settlement who are friends with her family."

"Will they attack us?"

"You, never. Me, yes. I'm sure they will try."

"Do you think you can take them? They don't look nearly as fit as you. Should we just avoid them by getting the police to escort us past them?"

"Parri males don't involve guards or others in our squabbles. And yes, I could win in a fight against those three." Suddenly, York felt sick inside. "But I don't want you to see that side of me, Sara. It might frighten you. Blood may be spilled."

She stepped in front of him and frowned, holding his gaze. "Tell me the truth. Can you really take those three in a fight? No male-pride bullshit."

He knew the word she used since it was one of Nara's favorites. "Easily. That's the truth."

Sara did the oddest thing—she smiled.

"Okay. Give me all the bags then." She held out her hands. "You kick their asses. I'll try to stay far enough away to avoid blood splatter. These are shelter clothes I'm wearing, though, so no biggie if that happens. All the new stuff you bought is protected in these sacks."

He gaped at her. She was *encouraging* him to fight? It didn't make sense.

She stepped closer, gripping the handles of the bags and tugging them from his hand. "Give."

He released them.

"I grew up in a very poor section of Earth, York. Remember when I said I hate being hit? Bullies targeted me all the time. And my mom...she, um, sometimes took boyfriends to make our lives better. Not a prostitute, exactly, but let's just say she used men on a regular basis to get better-paying jobs and housing for us. You aren't going to frighten me if you kick some ass. As a matter of fact, I respect you for standing up for yourself and protecting me. I'm no lightweight in a fight, either. I've been in plenty of them in my life. Just not against big blue guys. I'm smart enough to know they'd hand me my ass. Not you, though." She glanced up and down his body. "You're built like a fighting machine. Let's get this over with so we can go up to your ship."

"It won't frighten you to see me fight? Disgust you? Make you worry I'll harm you?"

"Not one bit."

He saw sincerity in her eyes, and finally grinned. "You are perfect, Sara."

"Just protect that pretty face of yours. You owe me a kiss since we got married. On my planet, that's what we do." She winked, grinning wider. "Be careful."

"Stay behind me." She thought he was pretty? Now he couldn't wait to take her up on that offer of a kiss. "I'll make this fast."

"Kick butt, York."

He stormed forward, hoping that Sara meant it.

Chapter Four

Sara was nervous but tried to mask the emotion from her face as she followed York. Nodo's father pointed at him the second he saw them coming, and the two men with him converged on her new bond mate.

York motioned for her to stop and stay back. She didn't hesitate to do just that. Those guys were big, and she didn't want to accidently get hit.

York looked really muscular, but did that actually mean he knew how to fight? She was about to find out.

Her body tensed, and she glanced around, looking for a anything that could be used as a weapon in case shit went bad. She came up with nothing. There weren't even any rocks scattered around the space port. Just smooth pavement.

The aliens around them looked excited when one of the Parri men yelled at York. "You can't do this to one of our women! And for what? *That?*" He jerked his head toward Sara. "It's hideous!"

She flinched at the insult, praying that wasn't true. Did she really look ugly to a Parri? She hoped her new man found her attractive.

Then York spoke, his voice more of a snarl, and his words soothed her. "Don't insult my beautiful Sara!"

"I demand you void your contract with that alien and bond to my daughter!" The older Parri got in York's face.

"No."

"No?" The older man sputtered—and threw a sucker punch.

York moved lightning fast and avoided the blow. He grabbed the elder Parri by his arm and shoved him back without otherwise harming him.

The other two Parri went nuts regardless, instantly attacking.

Sara gripped the bags tighter, prepared to start swinging. They had some heft to them, since York had insisted on not only buying her at least a dozen outfits, but also items like shoes and shampoos. She figured it might do some damage if she swung them at the bastards who didn't fight fair. Three to one odds were cowardly.

She took a step in their direction...before it became obvious York didn't need her help.

He threw a punch at one guy, knocking him on his ass, hard. The sound of the strike made her flinch, since she was pretty sure York had broken the guy's nose.

Parri blood was red, she discovered, watching a whole lot of it pour out of the downed guy's face.

York spun fast and kicked out, taking the second Parri down. That one was thrown so hard, he hit the pavement and almost flipped ass over end before crumpling.

Then Nodo's father jumped on York's back.

York crouched forward swiftly, sending the elder man flying over him. He landed with a painful grunt at York's feet. The one with the broken nose got up and tried to throw another punch. Her alien caught the man's fist in his hand and more bones popped. She only heard the noise for a split second before the Parri getting his fist crushed began to scream in agony.

York shoved him, putting him back on his ass.

Nodo's dad rolled over and got up, attempting once more to tackle York. Her bond mate didn't even try to avoid the large body coming at him, but instead kind of side-stepped, grabbed the man, and changed his direction. He released him fast, making him stumble into the still-downed second man. Their bodies tangled and both grunted, staying on the ground.

York crossed his arms over his chest. "Are you done? I have a shuttle to catch."

"You ohlta!" The one with the broken nose spit blood out of his mouth. "No honor!"

Part of the insult didn't translate to Sara's implant. It was probably for the best. The men stayed down, nursing their wounds, but shot vicious glowers at York. Sara approached, keeping a wide berth of the injured Parri to move to York's side.

"Nice work." She smiled at him. "You know what? Now I'm getting hungry. It's about lunchtime. Ready to go to your ship? I am."

He wiped his hands on his black uniform pants and took the bags from her. "Sounds good. I apologize for that, Sara."

"For what? You didn't lose." She winked.

He grinned back at her.

"You chose that ugly creature over my beautiful Nodo?"

York's face darkened a deep shade of blue, and he growled. "She is not ugly!"

Sara put her hand on his arm and faced the elder Parri. "Here's some advice. Maybe if your daughter could actually remember a guy's name and not treat him like shit, he'd be more inclined to bond with her. Good luck finding some idiot to take her off your hands. I think you're stuck with Nodo for life." She glared at the one with the broken nose. "And *you* have a lot of nerve accusing York of having no honor. The *three* of you jumped him. Ever heard of a fair fight? Look that up so you don't sound so stupid the next time you make wild accusations."

York smiled at her gently. "Let's go, Sara."

She nodded. York moved her ahead of him, his touch comforting, and put his big body between her and the males on the ground. It was a courteous, protective thing to do. It made her like York even more.

They didn't speak again until they'd reached an alien standing in front of a small shuttle.

He smiled and opened the door. "*The Vorge*, right?"

"Yes."

"I recognized the uniform. I took another party up hours ago."

York ushered her into the shuttle and got her seated, putting her bags on the floor. She remembered something then. "We forgot to pick up *your* things."

"I had my friend Dovis do that this morning. He and his mate stayed at the same hotel as I did last night."

"Oh." She belted in and York took a seat next to her. "Are you okay?"

He nodded, examining his hands quietly.

"Are you hurt?" She leaned forward, seeing some darker marks on his knuckles but no bleeding or torn skin.

"No. Embarrassed."

"For what? You totally handled those three men well."

"Parri have a reputation for being violent, and it makes females leery of us. Males tend to use fists to work out their differences with each other. We're barely bonded and already you've seen me in a fight." His gaze locked with hers. "You've been very nice and understanding about this, Sara. I appreciate it."

"Nice has nothing to do with it. Those guys were asking for trouble. Your restraint was amazing. You put them on the ground quickly instead of toying with them. I have a feeling you could have inflicted a lot of pain and damage if you'd wanted to. I'm not afraid of you, or put off by what just happened, York. I'm glad you can defend yourself."

A small smile curved his lips as the shuttle engines came on. They were loud enough to make talking impossible unless they wanted to shout. The craft lifted off the ground with astounding speed, and Sara reached over, clutching his thigh in fear.

York leaned close and put his arm around her, bending enough to press his lips to her ear. "It's fine. I forgot you aren't used to this."

She felt comforted by his hold and turned her head, putting her face against his chest. The shuttle shook a little and she turned toward him, latching on to his arm, too. It was a scary ride. They were hurtling into the sky at an alarming rate of speed.

York pressed a kiss to the top of her head, holding her more firmly. She dared to stare at the front, spotting the pilot and, beyond him, the open sky through the view windows. They were leaving Relon and heading into space.

When she'd been taken from Earth, the trip hadn't been pleasant. Of course, she'd been in a cage and the cargo hold hadn't had any windows. There'd just been a lot of motion, sound, and hanging on to bars for dear life. A padded seat with belts was a lot more comfortable.

And this time, her future looked better. She had York.

The rattling and shaking grew worse as they transitioned from the planet's atmosphere into space. The sky turned black and the interior lights automatically kicked on to keep them from sitting in the dark. She heard the pilot speaking but couldn't make out his words. Minutes later, she spotted a huge vessel.

York pointed to it, and then the insignia on his chest. She understood. That was *The Vorge*. It was huge and nice-looking, almost big enough to be considered one of those luxury cruise ships on Earth, only it flew in space.

And that would be her new home.

The pilot docked and shut down the engines. He rose from the front. "We're here. Thank you for flying with me."

York released her and they unbelted. He offered her a hand to help her up, and she was grateful for it, feeling oddly off balance. It was probably the difference between the gravity on the shuttle versus a planet. It had made her sick on the transport from Earth for the first hour.

"Are you well? You're pale."

"I'm not used to going from a planet and then not being on one."

"I understand. I've been traveling for three years now. You adjust to it." He got the bags and firmly took her arm. "Just lean on me, Sara. Do you want me to carry you?"

It was a sweet offer but she didn't want him to see her as totally weak. "I'll be fine."

The pilot let them out of the shuttle. She figured he'd already been pre-paid, since York didn't have to give him creds or place his hand on a pad. They entered a docking sleeve and stepped into a corridor on *The Vorge*. York led her through the ship to a lift, and then they got out on one of the floors.

She couldn't help but stare. The last transport she'd been on hadn't been nearly as nice. At least, not the part of it she'd gotten to see from the jail-like cage she'd been kept in.

York stopped at a door, released her, and pressed his hand to the surface. It opened, showing her a nice room that reminded her of a hotel suite. It had a small living area and a huge bed in the far corner. An open doorway revealed a bathroom.

"It's not much but it's ours," York murmured.

"It's really nice!" She'd lived in a hovel on Earth. Her apartment had been a third of the size and not nearly as clean or updated. The ceiling was a good ten feet high, too. Bright lighting showed off every inch. Not just two bulbs that tended to burn out often and need replacing—when she could afford it.

"Please, go in first."

She did, figuring he didn't know about the wedding custom on Earth of carrying his bride over the threshold, which was fine with her.

The furniture was modern, looked new, and appeared comfortable. She gawked a bit, taking in every inch of space. Not once did she ever think she'd get to live somewhere that big or clean. There weren't water stains on the walls or ceiling. No faint scent of mold. Her new home made her smile.

York drew her attention when the door sealed them inside, and he put down her bags. "I wish it was better for you."

She turned to him. "This is amazing, York."

He looked surprised.

"This is the nicest place I've ever been in. Trust me. My apartment building on Earth was hundreds of years old, and they didn't often do many repairs or upgrades on it. It was tiny and cramped. There were cracks in the walls from age. I love this!"

"I'm glad." His skin darkened. "I mean, not glad that you lived in such a place, but that you like our cabin."

She drew closer to him and put her hands on his chest. "I wasn't understating that I was very poor, York. All my life. I never had nice things or...well, many possessions at all. I think you bought me more new clothes today than I've been able to buy in my lifetime. I mostly got used things, since they were more affordable. I want you to know where I'm coming from. This," she paused to remember what he'd called it, "cabin, is a huge upgrade for me. I really love it. I'm not just being polite. I'm easy to impress." She winked. "Just so you know. Stop worrying so much."

He smiled, gently putting his hands on her hips. "I'm glad you're my bond mate."

"I am too."

He gently caressed her hips, and then cleared his throat. "Food. Right. Do you wish to eat here or with the crew? I don't want to overwhelm you, but they are going to want to meet you soon."

What if they hated her? She was human, and aliens didn't seem to like them.

Then she remembered what York had told her about his friends. They had chosen her kind to marry. Other humans would be onboard.

On the heels of that thought, new fears worried her. York had told her that Nara, the captain's woman, had left Earth and had owned a trade vessel. That must mean she'd come from money to be able to afford to that. What if she hated Sara for having been born in the slums? Thought she wasn't good enough for York? Mari might be more accepting, since she'd been a slave.

She wasn't ready to find out how the other two humans would react to her.

"Could we eat here for today? Maybe tomorrow you could introduce me to your crew?"

"Whatever makes you feel at ease, Sara. I want you to be happy with me."

"I am." He was such a sweetheart. She'd really lucked out. "On Earth, we have what's called a honeymoon. It's where the couple that gets married spends some days alone, kind of getting to know each other." She didn't mention the tons of sex, not sure she was ready to go there yet with York.

"I like that. We can bond and learn more about each other. I need to speak to my captain, though, and I'll bring us food. Will you be fine alone? Otherwise, I could call him to come here and ask Midgel to deliver lunch."

"You can go. I'll be fine on my own. Just tell me where to unpack the things you bought me and that'll keep me busy."

He released her hips and inched away. She dropped her hands from his chest and followed him across the room to the bed. There were hidden drawers and storage in the wall next to it. All the ones lower than York's waist were empty. That amused her. He probably didn't want to crouch down to get his underwear. She didn't mind.

The tour of the bathroom came next. He made sure she knew how to use everything in there and showed her where storage was located.

He hesitated before leaving. "Are you certain you will be fine alone? I won't be gone long."

He's so thoughtful. "I'm good, York. Promise."

He nodded. "I'll show you around *The Vorge* when you're ready. It's large."

That was probably a hint for her not to go snooping around on her own. "Maybe tomorrow. Today, I have no plans to leave our cabin."

He nodded. "I'll hurry." He stepped out of the bathroom and she trailed behind, watching as he left.

She walked over to the bags and picked them up, grinning as she once again admired her new living situation. There were even port windows, but they were currently closed. She'd have to figure out how to open them later. For a girl who never thought she'd see space, that would actually be her everyday view from now on.

York had focused his thoughts to the Pods, the trio of aliens who could read his mind, and asked them to have the crew meet him in the dining hall when he'd first come onboard *The Vorge*. He also asked them not to tell anyone that he'd taken a bond mate. That was news he wanted to share himself. He made his way there and found that they'd done as he'd asked. The crew was assembled, waiting for him.

"What's going on?" Cathian's nostrils flared as he sniffed. "I smell blood."

"He's been fighting again," Dovis snorted. "Nothing new, but this time I don't see *him* busted up any. It must not have been a brawl. Tell us if Relon has an arrest warrant out for you or if one is coming. We'll deal with it."

"Diplomatic immunity again?" Nara chuckled. "That's always a good excuse to keep you guys out of jail."

One of the three Pods giggled. Midgel, their timid cook, startled over the sound, and inched away from the trio.

Mari glanced at the others. "Is that really a thing?"

"Sure is," Marrow informed her. "We've had to clean up plenty of messes left behind by Raff. He tends to leave bodies, though, instead of just beaten-up adversaries."

Raff crossed his arms over his chest and smirked.

65

"I have an announcement." York stood straighter, staring at his crew and friends at their seated positions at the tables. "I have a bond mate."

They looked surprised. Cathian rose slowly to his feet. "What?"

"She's human." York grinned. "I met her on Relon. Her name is Sara."

Nara stood next. "Someone from Earth? Where is she?"

"In my cabin. She's shy, and said we should have a honeymoon before she meets all of you. I'll introduce you to her tomorrow."

One of the Pods giggled again. "She's willing. He did not buy her. And the blood isn't hers. He was in a fight with males who were angry he didn't choose a Parri female, instead."

York scowled, glaring at his crew. "Who thought that?"

No one admitted it.

"Whoever thought the blood was my Sara's, or thought I bought her at a slave house, is a shaft-head," York grumbled. "I feel insulted."

Cathian turned and stared at the Pods. They immediately sat straighter in their seats and locked their gazes on him. Long seconds ticked by as York waited. He wondered what his captain was saying to them, since he wasn't using words.

The Pod known as One spoke. "She's from Earth, is no threat, and she was the one to ask York to be her bond mate. She didn't like it on Relon. She thought York was a very nice male. He had picked a 'raging bitch' to be his bond mate at first—that's the phrase Sara uses when thinking of the female Parri—and she wanted to save York from being miserable."

York growled and stormed forward. *"Stop.* Don't read her mind or share her thoughts, One. It's rude! I haven't even told her about your kind yet, or that you can do that."

Cathian turned to face him. "Blame me. You went down to the surface during our time off and returned with a human. It makes me wary. I didn't even know you were looking for a bond mate."

"There's no need to be wary. I've been lonely. I didn't tell you because I wasn't certain if any female would be willing to accept me," York admitted. "Sara is a good human."

Cathian turned to stare at the pods.

"She *is* a good one," Two agreed. "Her thoughts are pleasant." He stared at York. "We can't help hearing what we do. Your Sara has good intentions, and she wishes for you to be happy together."

York couldn't be angry at that. It was actually a relief to know Sara hadn't just fooled him to get off Relon. The Pods would have told him if she'd deceived him. He nodded his thanks.

Three spoke next. "Sara has had a difficult time. She thinks often of how Earth betrayed and sold her. She believes York is her hero for saving her from the unpleasantness she dealt with on Relon. Not many aliens were kind to her, because she's human. She longs for a home and for someone to care about her. She hopes that male will be York, as she's already beginning to have strong feelings for him."

That news had warmth spreading through York's chest, and he grinned.

"Congratulations." Cathian came forward and embraced him. "We're happy for you."

"Only if she's not annoying," Dovis grumbled.

Mari shook her head at her mate. "Don't be grumpy."

"He's talking about me," Nara chuckled. "I hope she gives you hell, too, Dovis. You *are* a grumpy ass. It's good for you to have people call you on your bullshit."

Dovis growled. "You've called me fur face under your breath dozens of times. And muzzle mouth."

Nara just grinned. "Well, it's sometimes true."

York walked over to Midgel. "I don't plan to stay to watch them argue and tease each other. Can you prepare a meal for two that I can take to my quarters? Something a human would enjoy?"

The cook dipped her head in agreement. "Give me twenty minutes. I'll drop it off at your cabin. No need to wait. Be with your bond mate. I'm happy for you, York. I don't know why anyone would live with someone on purpose, but some aliens are weird."

He hid his smile. The cook wasn't one to be social. "Thank you." He fled before anyone could stop him.

Chapter Five

Sara finished her meal slowly. York ate faster than her, but he'd been attentive to her during lunch. He'd shared some boyhood stories of the trouble he and his friends had gotten into. She'd laughed plenty at their antics. He was funny as well as kind.

"Did you ever get into trouble as a child?" He peered at her curiously.

"All the time," she admitted. "Only I didn't pull funny pranks the way you and your friends did. It was more about revenge."

He smiled. "Tell me."

"You might not like me if I do."

"I doubt that's true. Test me, Sara. Have faith in your bond mate to be understanding."

"Okay." She used a cloth napkin to wipe her lips and put down her fork and knife. "My mom used to date his guy who hated me. He was horrible. I overheard him talking on his phone to a friend, saying he would convince my mother to abandon me. There was no way was he going to marry her if he had to take on her kid, too. All I could think about was how this jerk planned to steal my mom and I'd be homeless, starving on the streets."

"He could do that?" Anger deepened York's voice. "I would never abandon a child."

She hesitated. "I wasn't sure what my mom would do. He made good money and had a respectable job. She'd have had an easier life without me. Any child is a huge burden to a single parent, where I come from.

Anyway, it scared me bad enough that I implied there were three more kids she'd hidden from him, my siblings, and that she was only dating him to fool him into marriage. He stopped seeing her right after."

She tensed, watching his expression, hoping he didn't think she was a horrible person.

He nodded. "That was smart."

The tension in her body eased slightly. "I felt bad. My mom was depending on him to make our lives easier. I was more afraid of losing her, though, to be honest. She was the only person I had to depend on and who loved me. I don't think I'd have survived long on the streets on my own as a child. It was hard enough as an adult. We lived together until the day she died, sharing an apartment and bills. On Earth, most people need to team up with someone to have a decent home and three meals a day."

York leaned closer and held out his hand. "You will never be alone again, Sara. I'm here now."

Tears threatened to rise but she blinked them back, deeply touched. She took his hand. "Thank you."

"Bond mates are forever. I will spend the rest of our lives showing you how much you matter to me. You'll never grow hungry or know struggle. I promise you that. Cathian said if he ever retires, the crew is welcome to make a home on his planet. I doubt he will, though, for a very long time. He's the first Tryleskian to not step down from his ambassador duties after taking a mate. *The Vorge* is our home." He motioning to the room. "If we are ever blessed with children, we'll expand into other cabins near us for bedrooms. Cathian did that already, when he life-locked to Nara. They plan to have a litter when he goes into his next heat cycle."

"A litter? I think you mentioned that before, but I didn't fully understand."

"Tryleskians usually have more than one infant at a time. I've only heard of a single birth happening once. That's Raff, another crew member. He and Cathian are cousins. Cathian is from a litter of three. He has two brothers who were born with him."

It didn't shock her that some aliens had multiple babies. Humans sometimes had twins or triplets. She'd just wondered how many made up a litter. "What about Parri?"

"Single births. Two infants are rare for our kind."

She felt a bit of relief. To birth one of his babies would probably be difficult enough. "He'd let us expand our cabin if I ever get pregnant?"

"Of course. Cathian has told all of us that if we decide to have children, we can expand, and that he hoped we'd stay on *The Vorge*. The crew is family. We stick together."

"That's really great. Most bosses hate when a worker gets pregnant."

"Cathian is more than a boss. We're a band of outcasts. Some emotionally and a few literally."

"Can you explain?"

"My planet had to be evacuated because it was dying. The surface could no longer support life, so I have no home to return to. Dovis's people were cruel to him, and he fled to live in space. He never wants to return. Midgel was seen only as a breeder by her people, to birth more of

71

her race. She allowed it to happen twice but refuses to do it again. She just wants to live alone in peace. *The Vorge* allows her to do so. Marrow was born on a planet where the females are subservient to males. She fled to avoid an arranged marriage to a controlling shaft-head. Her words. On her planet, females aren't allowed to work or given a say in what they do with their lives. Now she has freedom. And Raff grew up on a hostile planet he hated, abandoned by his Tryleskian father, and survived by having to kill or be killed. He was alone after his mother died, but now he has us."

"That's so sad." She felt bad for the crew members. It seemed like all of them had endured rough upbringings and circumstances that had led them to *The Vorge*.

"Nara left Earth to be the captain of a shuttle for trade. She had reasons for leaving Earth, but I don't know them. She doesn't ever want to return there, now that she's fallen in love with Cathian. Her place is by his side. And Mari was sold into slavery by her parents. She was raised working on a repair station, and this ship is her first and only true home. She wants to be with Dovis, and seems very happy now. Cathian himself left his home to avoid being forced into a loveless marriage to breed the next generation for his family. He would have hated that. Instead, he met Nara and fell in love. As for the Pods, they were sold by their own people as well, and they feel it would never be safe to return to their planet.

"We're all like you, Sara. *The Vorge* is our sanctuary. The crew is our family. It's where we all belong and are happiest together. Did I explain that well?"

"Yes, very well."

"And now *you're* a part of this family."

The tears threatened to flow again, and she had to blink once more. "Thank you."

"Thank you for offering to be my bond mate."

She grinned. "I'm much better than Nagway."

He chuckled. "In every way."

She made a decision in that very moment. York had offered her time to get to know him better before they became intimate...but why put it off? He was incredibly respectful, and she liked him. He was sexy—for a big blue guy with fangs—and she'd committed to him for life. There was no sense in waiting.

She stood and locked her gaze with his.

"York...I'm nervous about bonding, but...let's get naked." She smiled.

His eyes widened and his mouth parted.

It was clear that was the *last* thing he'd expected her to say.

"We don't have to rush things, Sara."

She hadn't considered that *he* might not be ready to have sex yet. "Do you not want me?" She wasn't overly tall at five foot seven, or blue like the Parri, and certainly less muscular than Nodo.

Oh God. Maybe he thought humans were hideous, too.

"Do you find me unattractive?"

He stood and motioned to the front of his pants. "What do you think?"

She glanced down and saw the tight uniform outlining a thick, large cock. He was definitely hard.

The picture the Relon instructor had shown her on the pad flashed in her memory. It seemed to be accurate. York was much bigger than a human.

"I am definitely attracted to you, and I find you beautiful, Sara. I just don't want you to feel rushed or think you must quickly bond to me. Only the two of us will know if you need more time. And when the time comes, I want you to want *me* as much as I do you."

She tore her attention from the front of his pants and met his gaze. He had to be the only man she'd ever met who was that considerate. Most guys would have been all over her if she'd said "get naked" to anyone else. And York was worried about her feeling rushed into being with him.

It only strengthened her resolve to get him into bed.

"I want you, York. Am I still nervous? Yes. Of course. You're bigger than me." She glanced down at the front of his pants. "That's a bit scary...but we'll go slow." It would be a problem if his cock was too large to fit inside her without pain. She backed up and smiled again. "We can at least fool around. You owe me a kiss, remember? I heard Parri like skin-to-skin contact."

He stepped around the table. "We need it," he corrected, his voice turning huskier. "Will that bother you? I'll want to hold you when we sleep, without anything between us."

She backed her way to the bed and began to strip. "I've always wanted a man who likes to cuddle."

"I'll be that man."

She found that sexy. *Everything* about York was sexy. Her mind flashed to the few boyfriends she'd had. There hadn't been many. Most men had been jerks to her, since she wasn't exactly gorgeous. She'd also had to deal with a few bosses who'd implied she might get more hours and better pay if she dropped to her knees and blew them. The only physical contact she'd wanted with those assholes involved punching them in their mouths or kicking them in the balls.

The three men she'd dated had turned into disasters. Each of them had implied they had feelings for her but, in the end, she'd just been a body to use for as long as they could fool her into believing their lies. All three had been sleeping with other women, who they were lying to as well.

York wasn't the type to play mind games or see how many women he could string along to gain bragging rights over to his buddies. The more she thought about it, the more she liked that he was an alien. Human men had never been good to her.

She just hoped the sex was better with York. Her boyfriends had been nothing for her to brag about.

New life, new experiences. She was up for that.

Sara pushed the thoughts of her past away and climbed naked onto the bed, rolled to her back, and worked up the courage to gaze at York. He was her future.

She swallowed hard. He had stripped out of his clothes, too, and stood at the edge of his massive bed. His skin was blue everywhere, which she was starting to love. It was an attractive shade that she found

75

soothing. He had tons of muscles and the best physique she'd ever seen. So big...but that didn't scare her. She already knew he could be gentle.

Her focus lowered down his flat stomach to appreciate the ripples of muscles there as well. Her eyes widened a bit when she studied his cock. It was a slightly darker shade than the rest of his skin. He was long and wide. The shape of it was slightly different from the few human dicks she'd seen. The tip reminded her of a bulb, slightly rounder than the shaft, but not by much.

What surprised her were the bumps that ran along the top of his shaft all the way to the root. That wasn't something she'd noticed in the picture of the naked Parri the instructor had shown her.

"Am I frightening to you?"

His husky voice drew her gaze to his face. "We're going to have to go slow. You're big, that's for sure."

"My friends have had lots of sex with their humans. They'd have warned me if there was a problem. I won't hurt you, Sara."

"I take it that you've never done this before? Sex with my kind, I mean."

He shook his head. "I did research on humans when Nara was brought onboard. I like to help Dovis with security. It was important to know if she'd be a danger to Cathian in any way while he was vulnerable in heat. He's much bigger and stronger than her, but he wasn't thinking clearly. Part of that research included anatomy." He licked his lips. "I was curious, and I read up on everything in our ship's database about sex with a female of your race. You have a button that is very sensitive."

Button? She quickly realized what he meant...and decided to be brazen.

She bent her legs up and spread them apart to give him a clear view. "You mean my clit?" She slid her hand down her stomach to point it out. "This. It's *very* sensitive."

She couldn't miss the way his hard cock jerked, giving her a tiny wave. A low rumble of a growl escaped from him, and he put his knee on the bed, coming at her slowly. He bent forward, bracing himself on his hands, and stared at her sex.

"You're very small and pink." His nostrils flared. "You smell so good..."

Butterflies fluttered in her belly and her heart rate increased as he lowered even more, getting his face up close and personal with her girl parts. "I'll stretch a bit. Women do that. You know, to fit you inside me."

With his longer hair falling forward and his head dipped, she could no longer see his cock. It was probably for the best, since she wanted to focus on other things besides how it would work out when they got to that point.

She reached up and brushed her fingers over his shoulders, before running them down his biceps. His skin was warm and soft, but hard at the same time. Firm.

"Can I touch you here, Sara?"

"Yes." He seemed fascinated with her pussy. At least he hadn't made some kind of displeased expression or averted his gaze. She wondered if she was very different from a Parri female. At some point, she'd try to look up that information if it was available.

York made another low growling noise, and she tensed when his warm breath fanned her slit.

An instant later, a thick, wet tongue licked at her clit.

She sucked in a sharp breath. His tongue felt a little raspy, and as he licked her again, she realized his cock wasn't the only thing that had bumps. She could feel them as he ran his tongue along her clit.

The pleasure flooded her.

"That feels so good," she encouraged.

He did it again and again, growing a bit more aggressive. Sara moaned and let her fingers slide into his silky hair. He growled, adding some vibrations, and she moaned louder.

He adjusted his body a little, the bed shifting slightly, and his hand lightly caressed her inner thigh, inching higher.

Sara threw back her head and whispered his name when he slid one of his fingers inside her pussy.

She was wet, obviously, since his thick digit pushed inside her without trouble, going deep. He had good-sized fingers, and just one felt pretty amazing. He slowly began to fuck her with his finger, moving in and out.

She wiggled her hips, knowing she was about to come.

"Don't stop! I'm almost there," she panted.

He grew even more aggressive with his licks, occasionally sucking on her clit with his hot mouth. His finger drove in and out of her faster.

That was it.

Sara cried out his name, her eyes squeezing shut as her world imploded in ecstasy.

A loud snarl came from York. She heard him, but it took her seconds to even try to open her eyes. The bed moved again and his finger withdrew, then he pulled his mouth away from her clit.

"You're very wet. Are you ready for me, bond mate?"

She nodded, finally opening her eyes. "Yes."

He came down on top of her body, making certain he didn't crush her. He had to weigh a lot more than her, but he braced his arms and held himself up easily. She adjusted her legs, wrapping them loosely around his waist as he positioned his hips.

Their gazes locked. He had incredibly beautiful eyes, and she noticed for the first time that there were some yellow flecks of color in his irises, reminding her of streaks of golden sunshine reflecting on a blue sea.

"I'll be gentle and slow."

His voice had grown so deep, it gave her the good kind of chills. She let her fingers slide through his hair then cupped his face, lifting her head. He glanced at her lips and leaned closer.

She closed her eyes as their mouths touched. His lips were full and velvety soft. But firm. Everything about York was firm. She licked his lower lip, and then sucked on it a little. He groaned, opening his mouth to her. She kissed him deeper.

He hesitated when her tongue met his, and Sara could taste herself on him, but then he met her move for move.

York could *kiss*.

He adjusted his lower body and she spread her legs wider to accommodate his hips. The head of his cock pressed against her pussy. She wiggled a little, getting him right where she ached, and then tightened her hold around his hips.

He pushed forward slowly.

His cock felt incredibly thick, but she was wet enough that he eased inside her sex. She felt her body stretching to take him.

He broke the kiss, growling low, and froze above her.

She opened her eyes, staring into his.

"You're so tight...hot. I don't want to hurt you."

"I can take you. You feel incredible."

He surged forward, entering her all the way, and stilled again.

Sara's body adjusted to his large size, and she'd never felt so full. A slight smile curved her lips. "Told you we'd make this work. Now move, baby."

He hesitated for only a second before withdrawing slightly, and then he started to rock.

Those bumps along the top of his cock suddenly took on new meaning.

Sara threw her head back again, having to close her eyes at how good each one of those bumps felt, hitting all the places inside her that she didn't even realize she had. One bump in particular made her clit throb harder, and as he fucked her faster, she had to cling to him.

Her second climax struck hard and fast.

York watched Sara's face and clenched his teeth together. He wanted to bite her so much, his fangs ached. She was so tight, and when she screamed out his name, her pussy clamped hard around his shaft. It nearly hurt. It was too good.

He lost it, feeling his seed leave his balls, and then white-hot rapture took all thought away.

He buried his face against her shoulder and bit. Not hard enough to hurt, but he wanted to leave his mark. Sara was *his*.

He remembered not to collapse on his small bond mate and crush her. She was fragile. Then he caught his breath and smiled when she looked at him.

Luck had been with him when he'd met Sara, and especially when she'd saved him from Nodo. He couldn't see feeling this kind of rightness if the Parri female were under him.

Sara was special. Perfect to him.

"Forever," he swore. "I will make sure you are always as happy as I am at this moment."

Sara reached up and ran her fingers through his hair. It felt good. No one had ever done that to him before. She trailed her hands down the strands to his shoulders, before caressing him there. Her touches were soft and soothing.

He gently eased his softening shaft from her tight pleasure spot, rolling back and taking her with him until she curled up to his side. It felt perfect when she rested her cheek on his chest.

"Our sex life is going to be fantastic."

81

He chuckled at her panted words. "Yes. It will be." He touched her skin, exploring her. She was so soft and silky. The sight of his blue body against her pale one appealed to him. She didn't feel alien to him anymore. Only...his.

"I like holding you and being this close."

She snuggled tighter against him. "Me too. I have a feeling cuddling is going to be one of our favorite pastimes as a couple."

"I look forward to it."

"Want to do that again?"

He chuckled. "Let's catch our breath first, and then I plan to explore every inch of you."

"Only if I can explore you, too."

His grin widened. "You're the perfect bond mate, Sara."

"So are you, York." She paused. "I liked the bite."

He had hoped she wouldn't notice that loss of control. "I apologize. I know humans don't do that. I read a lot on the subject."

"Well, if you haven't noticed, we're not a human couple—and the bite was *hot*." She held his gaze. "You can do that to me anytime."

He checked her skin. "There's going to be a small bruise from my fangs. I didn't cause you to bleed."

"Your love bites feel amazing. I'm not worried about you nicking my skin." Her gaze lowered to his mouth. "The fangs are sexy, York. Everything about you is sensual to me."

He grinned. "You are the same to me, my Sara. And I shall bite you often."

Chapter Six

Sara was nervous about meeting the crew. They were all assembling for dinner together, and she wondered what a dining hall would look like on a space vessel. She'd never been anywhere so nice, but *The Vorge* continued to remind her of one of those luxury cruise liners she'd seen tons of ads for in her previous life. It had always been a dream of hers to go on a cruise, but they were out of her price range.

"They will love you," York assured her, wrapping his arm around her waist to pull her close to his side.

"You keep saying that, but humans are weird. We tend to come from different social circles. I'm not too worried about the ex-slave, but the captain's wife had enough money to leave Earth and buy her own shuttle. I've never met a rich person who tolerated someone beneath their station. They tend to avoid speaking to us, or even looking at us."

"Nara is nice. There are no social circles here."

She nodded, trying to relax as they made their way down a wide corridor. "My other concern are the Pods. They can really read my mind?"

"You'll like them. They don't normally share other's thoughts unless the captain is worried about someone being a danger."

She noticed how his voice deepened a little, and she picked up a hint of anger in it. "Did that happen with you?" She peered up at him.

He met her gaze. "I promise, you'll like the Pods. Just don't compare them to Hampy Dampy."

"What's that?"

"I don't know, but it upsets them when Nara teases them. Something about an Earth children's book or passed-down story."

She must not have read or heard that story. "I'll remember that."

The double doors in front of them slid open to reveal a large room with several tables. The sight of people sitting at them silently had Sara pressing her lips together and forcing a smile. Anxiety gripped her again as she got a glimpse of at least five different kinds of aliens.

York's hold on her tightened even more, as if he was afraid she'd try to flee.

A large alien stood, facing them. He was tall and muscular, with wild blond hair. He had a human-like body, but his eyes were all cat. They looked like the Earth's version of a lion. She tore her gaze away, seeing another one like him sitting in the far corner at a table by himself. He just peered at her with golden eyes surrounded by his own mane of blond hair. Those two must be the captain and his cousin. York had prepared her for meeting everyone by giving her their descriptions.

The three identical aliens were the Pods. They reminded her of eggs that happened to have arms and legs, with their white skin and rounded bodies.

Humpty Dumpty. Not Hampy Dampy. Now she understood.

One of the Pods snorted and twisted his body a little, staring at a human woman. That had to be Nara.

Nara lifted her hands. "Why are you glaring at me now? What did I do?"

Sorry, Sara thought at the Pods, tearing her attention from them. It was going to take her some time to adjust to knowing those three could always read her mind. It left her a little uncomfortable but York had explained they couldn't really help it. The Pods' abilities were like breathing to them.

Midgel looked like a human, if it had bred with a mouse. She was a tiny thing, probably weighing ninety pounds max, with dark hair and a pushed-out nose that had whiskers. It was that feature—and her pointed ears—that gave her the mousey look.

The woman ducked her head, avoiding eye contact. York had warned that the cook was extremely shy, and not one to talk unless necessary.

The female pilot openly studied her.

A bit of jealousy rose in Sara, making her chest feel tight. York had admitted he and Marrow used to have casual sex from time to time. It had ended after Cathian and Nara had gotten together. He'd assured her they were just friends, and there were no romantic feelings between them.

Marrow had a very thin coat of brown fur, and she was tall, muscular, and pretty. It amazed Sara that York had been attracted to such very different types of women. Then again, he was nothing like *her* ex-boyfriends.

The last couple had to be Dovis and Mari. He wasn't in fur today. She knew Dovis could change forms. She'd been shocked by the news; shapeshifters were real in space! Currently, she was grateful he didn't look like a werewolf standing on two legs. York said Nara frequently called Dovis "Wolfman" when he sported a muzzle, but at that moment, he resembled a human, though not completely. He was bigger, his features a bit harsher, and no one would mistake him as someone from Earth.

The human woman seated next to him was thin with long hair...and she was smiling at her. Mari also gave her a tiny wave.

Sara lifted her free hand to wave back. Her gaze returned to Nara, and she found the captain's wife smiling at her, too. That seemed to be a good sign.

"Another human! Woohoo! We're taking over the ship," Nara chuckled.

The captain turned, staring at her. "Really?"

"Okay, so aliens still outnumber us, but we're getting closer." Nara turned her head, addressing Marrow. "Tag, you're it. You have to find a human mate."

Marrow snorted. "No."

"We're totally cool," Nara responded. "Once you go human, you never want anything else. Your male crewmates will swear to that. Just ask them."

Marrow shook her head. "Nope. And Raff would probably kill a human. Wouldn't you, Raff?"

Sara's gaze instantly went to the silent lion man seated alone.

He shrugged. "Maybe a male, if he annoyed me, but pretty much everyone avoids me. As for the females, I can't see a human not running for her life if she saw *me* coming. I wouldn't kill a female but she might die from a heart attack."

"And that's as many words as we're going to get from him today," Dovis muttered. "Thanks for wasting them, Marrow." He stared at Sara. "Raff doesn't talk much. Don't take it personal. Welcome to *The Vorge*."

"That was my line." The captain, Cathian, came forward and offered his hand. "Hello, Sara. I congratulated your bond mate already on your union, but I'd like *you* to hear it from me as well. We're very glad that you've joined our crew."

She shook his large hand, feeling intimidated as hell. This was York's boss, as well as his friend. It was his ship. "Thank you. It's an honor to meet you all."

Nara got up and came to his side. She stuck out her hand. "So, straight from Earth, huh? Is it still a shitball?"

Sara shook her hand. "You could say that. The government has decided to get rid of women like me by trading us for alien technology." She'd decided to be honest with her fellow humans from the start.

"Women like you?" Nara asked, her expression sobering. "I know English is commonly spoken all over Earth now, but you sound American. Are you?"

Sara nodded. "I'm from a poverty-stricken district on the West Coast," she explained, waiting to see how the woman would react. "They're rounding up low-income women without families and shipping us off."

"Those jerks! I can't say I'm surprised, unfortunately. You're better off here." Nara's smile returned. "You're going to be happy on *The Vorge*. Tons of food. Great people. Fun adventures." Her expression softened as she glanced up at York. "And you married a sweetie." She held Sara's gaze. "Good job."

Sara felt tears prick her eyes and she blinked them back. "Thanks. He's wonderful. I'm lucky we met."

York gently squeezed her waist. "I'm the lucky one."

"The food is getting cold." Midgel stood. "No complaints if it is. I'll serve. Stay out of my kitchen." The tiny alien marched toward a doorway but paused, glancing back at Sara. "We like you. York made sure we knew to tell you." Then she fled.

York sighed. "That's Midgel."

Nara nodded. "She's as socially awkward as hell, but man, can that woman cook. You're going to enjoy her food."

Mari and Dovis came forward next.

The ex-slave hugged Sara, surprising her. She had a sweet smile. "You're going to love it here. I was super nervous when I came onboard, but I'm happy to report that it's the best thing to ever happen to me. Everyone is so nice."

Raff snorted loudly.

"Even him," Mari added. "Don't be fooled by his glares and the fact he doesn't talk much. He helped Dovis and I work out some problems we had." She lowered her voice conspiratorially. "He likes to play matchmaker."

A low growl came from Dovis.

Mari reached down and stroked his hand. "He *did* send me to the bridge to fix something."

"But nothing was broken. He fooled us both." Dovis took a deep breath and blew it out. "It ended very well." He lifted her hand to his lips, kissing it. "Raff can live."

Everyone peered at Raff. He smiled. It gave Sara chills. He might look a lot like Cathian, but there was a certain coldness in his golden eyes, instead of the warmth she saw in his cousin's. She silently promised to avoid him when York wasn't nearby. Not that she thought Raff would hurt her, but he sure was intimidating.

"Let's eat," Cathian announced. "Tell us all about you, Sara. We'll do the same. It's the best way to get to know each other."

Her nervousness returned but York took her hand. He was at her side, right with her, and he made her feel safe.

* * * * *

York loved the sound of Sara's laughter. It had taken a good half hour before his bonded mate had finally warmed to the crew. She no longer clung to his hand or scooted closer to his body. She was at ease.

He glanced around the table that most of them shared, feeling deep appreciation. He knew Nara and Mari would have a lot in common with Sara, despite their different backgrounds. They were the same race and had faced similar trials, living away from others of their kind.

Cathian was going out of his way to appear friendly. Even Dovis was giving it a shot, but York knew that was due to Mari. His mate encouraged him to be nicer and more outgoing with others.

Midgel had fled back to the kitchen as soon as possible, but the Pods and even Raff had hung out after the meal was finished. Of course, Raff sat at another table just watching them and listening to their conversation, but the fact that he'd stayed showed respect for Sara.

Marrow, on the other hand, was beginning to make him nervous with the way she kept frowning at him.

He finally excused himself, stating he was going to refill his drink. He pointedly stared at Marrow. She followed him across the room with her own empty cup.

"What is the matter with you?" He poured himself some juice, making sure to keep his voice soft enough that it didn't travel to anyone else.

"I'm just surprised that you went down to that planet and came back with a woman. You didn't warn any of us first that you planned to bring a bonded mate back with you. You'd think you'd mention that fact. We're supposed to be close friends."

He scowled, facing her. "Warn?"

She sighed. "You were my backup plan if I didn't find a mate in a year or two. It's irritating that you're no longer an option."

"Backup plan?"

"You know, if I couldn't find a mate, I'd ask *you*."

It was his turn to be surprised. "You don't have those feelings for me, Marrow." He didn't want to hurt her by reminding her they'd shared physical attraction, but nothing beyond that. Then again, she'd pointed that very thing out to him once. "We'd have made terrible bond mates. You find me too nice, and it annoys you. You've talked about the kind of male you're seeking, and it's nothing like who I am."

"You're right, but still, I figured we had decent sex. I knew you'd stick with me if we mated, and not be a controlling shaft-head."

He attempted to hide his flinch over being called "decent" in bed. Then again, the sex hadn't been anything near as intense as it was with his Sara. He had deep feelings for his human. He suspected he was falling in love with her, if he wasn't already.

"That's no reason to pick a male, Marrow. Besides, while we were occasionally having sex, you kept trying to tempt the other males on our crew into your bed, as well. What we had was never serious."

"True. I'm not hurt. Just surprised...and a little scared. What if I don't find a male who's right for me? We at least get along, and you're nice to me. That's always been a fear of mine, ending up with someone cruel. My mother was miserable. You know that, York. I told you that my father treated her like a servant. Then again, at least she *had* a mate. Perhaps I should have stayed and given the male my father chose for me a chance."

He sighed, pouring water for her. "Marrow, Sara makes me feel many wonderful things. You deserve that, too, when you find the right male. You shouldn't settle just because you feel you're reaching an age where you should already be mated. Leave your past behind you. You escaped your planet for a reason, remember? They'd have married you off the day you reached maturity, to a male who had no regard for your happiness or wishes. He'd have stifled you."

"It's just hard to see how happy the couples are. Now, I see you with Sara... You never once looked at *me* that way. I feel as if I'm missing out on something important. I'll be the only one left not mated."

"That's not true. Midgel never wants to be touched or even talked to. Raff certainly isn't the type to life-lock to a female." He glanced toward the table. "The Pods don't join with others. They self-produce if they wish to have young."

Marrow sighed. "It's just tough seeing the three of you happy, when I'm not."

"I understand. Believe me, I do. It's why I went to the surface looking for a bond mate. I was blessed to have found Sara. Keep contacting planets and talking to males. One day, you'll find a male who's right for you and makes you feel everything you're missing. Perhaps it will be soon."

"The dating agencies keep sending me bad matches. I speak to them on comms but they're all assholes. They're looking for females to keep their homes nice, and they're horrified that I wish to remain a pilot instead of popping out a ton of babies for them. Perhaps I need to search everywhere we stop myself to find the right male."

"You'll find him. I never thought I'd be lucky enough to be with a female like Sara, but it happened."

Marrow smiled. "Thanks. I feel better. I do like her, York. She looks at you the same way you do her. You matter to her. I'm glad that you found each other."

He grinned. "Thank you. You're a good friend."

He walked away, realizing that Sara watched him with a worried expression on her face. He understood. He would also feel uneasy if he saw her talking to someone she'd once been intimate with. Jealousy rose just thinking about that situation. He gave her a wink, hoping she wasn't experiencing the same jealousy. There was no reason for it. Sara had already become his heart.

He retook his seat next to her and leaned over, kissing her forehead.

She whispered, "Is everything okay?"

"I was telling Marrow how lucky and grateful I am that you're mine. She's happy for us. I was encouraging her to find the perfect male for her. It's tough to see couples happy together when one is alone."

The concern left her eyes and she leaned against him, her hand taking his under the table. They laced their fingers together. "I remember you telling me how you felt, seeing your friends mated. Maybe we can help her find a guy."

He chuckled. "I think it's best if Marrow finds her own male. She's determined."

Sara glanced over at Marrow and smiled at her. York appreciated that his bond mate cared about the well-being of his friends. She was everything a mate should be and more.

An hour later, he made excuses and they left. At the lift, he surprised her by scooping her into his arms. She laughed, wrapping her own arms around his neck.

"What are you doing?"

"Carrying you to bed. Nara said it's an Earth tradition. We're still on our honeymoon."

Chapter Seven

Sara moaned, her hands fisting the bedding. York had her bent over in front of him, on all fours, and was fucking her from behind, fast and hard. He felt amazing. He'd already gotten her off twice and was going for a third time. Sex with a big blue alien was way better than she'd ever hoped for or dreamed of.

His hands tightened on her hips as he fucked her even harder...

That was it. She cried out his name, seeing stars when her eyes closed. Her arms nearly collapsed under her as she felt him coming, too, snarling her name as he did. He slowed his thrusts until he remained still, buried inside her.

"This is a good morning, my beautiful Sara."

"That it is."

He eased his cock out of her body and collapsed onto his side next to her on their bed. She turned her head as he opened his arms. She didn't hesitate to snuggle into him.

He really *did* love to cuddle and hold her. Sleeping with him was like having a living, breathing blanket wrapped around her. His favorite position was spooning, and she had no complaints about using his arm for a pillow.

"I guess we won't be nullifying our marriage."

He tensed against her and his eyes widened.

She chuckled. "You should see your face right now. That was a joke. You know...we totally exchanged fluids before the three days were up."

He slid his hand to her side and tickled her. She laughed, trying to roll away. York came down on top of her, pinning Sara under him. He was always careful not to put too much of his weight on her.

"That wasn't funny. You're mine forever, bond mate. I never want to think about losing you. It would break me inside, and I wouldn't recover. You're everything to me, my Sara."

He melted her heart with his sincerity as she stared into his blue eyes. "You won't lose me. Not ever. You're stuck with me."

"I'm grateful to hear that. Would you like a tour today of *The Vorge* or shall we spend the entire day in bed?"

"It's nice that the crew is splitting your shifts to give you some more time off."

"They all realize it's important that we bond. I'm already feeling the physical effects."

"What physical stuff? The fact that we're having a lot of sex?"

"I told you that Parri bodies experience chemical changes. I'm undergoing my own."

She'd almost forgotten. "How do you know?"

"I feel them. It's difficult to explain...but my seed is thicker. Haven't you noticed?"

She hadn't. "You can get me pregnant now?"

He grinned. "It usually takes a few weeks but then I will be fertile."

A baby. She swallowed hard. It had been almost a year since she'd last been physical with a man on Earth. Contraceptives were an expense she hadn't been able to afford on her own. A couple usually split the cost to avoid an unplanned pregnancy. She wasn't currently on anything to prevent one.

"Don't panic, Sara. You have that look." He shifted his body, his fingers brushing her hair back from her face. He stroked her cheek with his thumb. "I did research while you were still sleeping this morning. Humans have birthed healthy Parri babies. Not many, but there are a few who have come forward with information. The females had no difficulties, despite the shorter pregnancy span of my race."

So someone else had done it before. That was great to know. "Shorter?"

"It stated humans have a normal birth at forty weeks. Parri are born in twenty-eight weeks."

Her eyes widened.

"Parri babies are usually born smaller than humans." He paused, frowning. "It said humans are nine yentas at birth, on average. Parri are seven yentas. Our growth spurts happen after leaving the mother's body."

"What is a yenta?"

"The size of a baby."

She let that information play in her head. That didn't sound so bad. Maybe yentas were pounds? If so, she could handle a seven-pound baby. She'd been worried they'd be closer to fifteen, considering how big York was. The shorter pregnancy span was a relief, too. Maybe it accounted for the smaller size of the babies.

"The babies were born healthy and the mothers did well." York sounded unconcerned. "It will be fine."

"Do you think our baby will look like you or me?"

He released her and rolled out of bed to grab a data pad off the living area table. He returned to their bed, switching the device on. He lay on his stomach and she stretched out on hers next to him. He pulled up two side-by-side pictures of babies.

Her breath caught in her lungs at the sight.

She was finally able to speak once her emotions stopped choking her. "They're amazingly adorable. Oh, York! Look how cute they are!"

He chuckled. "They are. This one has very pale-blue skin, almost closer to your color than mine. Look at his eyes. Those are human in shape but with the Parri blue. And this female infant was born with her mother's coloring, but Parri eyes and her father's white hair. Their children share features of each."

"It's the best of both worlds. Or should I say, races."

Then he showed her pictures of the two couples who'd had those babies, each set of proud-looking parents holding their child. "These are the only two couples who allowed their information to be uploaded. There are likely more. Most probably wanted to keep their privacy." He set the data pad down and peered at her. "We would have adorable young, Sara. Will you think about it? Otherwise, I should take you to visit the medical android. There's an implant he can give you to prevent my seed from creating a baby inside you until you're ready."

She chewed on her bottom lip as her gaze kept going to the picture on the pad. She'd always wanted a baby but had given up that dream after her repeated failed relationships on Earth. No way would she have had one on her own and subject it to the kind of childhood she'd had without a father.

York had changed all that.

"What do you want?" She stared at him, watching him closely.

"I want you to be happy."

"I know that. I want you to be happy, too. Be honest, York. Do you want to try for a baby?"

He hesitated.

"Tell me. Please?"

"I would love to have babies with you. I'd like to have one soon, but only when you're ready. I would be willing to wait until you feel more secure."

She took a deep breath and blew it out. "How about we leave it to chance? Just...see what happens?"

He grabbed her and collapsed onto his back, taking her with him. They almost crushed the data pad when he settled her on top of his body. She shoved it to the side, away from them.

A huge grin spread across his lips. "I like that. We'll leave it up to fate. After all, it brought me *you*."

She cupped his face and wiggled higher up his big frame, kissing him. Her body instantly responded. York always turned her on. He was a master at kissing, teasing her with his mouth and tongue. She really loved those bumps he had.

His cock hardened between them, and she spread her legs, straddling him.

A loud buzz sounded. Sara startled, jerking up and breaking the kiss. "Who has the worst timing ever to come visit us?"

York gripped her hips, lifted her off him, and crawled to the side of the bed to stand. "It must be Midgel with breakfast. Cover up."

She scrambled to yank the blankets over her body as York pulled on pants. He strode across their cabin and opened the door.

It wasn't the cook with a tray, though. It was Cathian.

"We need to talk."

"You gave me time off." York blocked most of the door. "Sara and I are bonding."

"I was just contacted by Rex."

"Your father's assistant? Is there an urgent Tryleskian issue we must address? Are they sending us somewhere on a mission?"

"I need to speak to you and Sara, along with some of the others. Get dressed and meet me in my office in ten minutes."

"What's going on?"

Sara became alarmed at York's tone—and the captain's. Something was wrong.

"Ten minutes," Cathian said.

York closed the door and turned. Their gazes met.

"What's happening?"

York came to her fast. "I don't know. Let's go find out."

* * * * *

99

York felt concern. Sometimes *The Vorge* was sent on hazardous missions when Cathian had to negotiate peace between his planet and another. It had never bothered him before, but now he had a bond mate. Sara was onboard. Their vessel was heavily armed, they could hold their own...but he hated the idea of her being in danger.

He kept a firm hold on Sara's hand as he led her to Cathian's office. She appeared afraid, despite his assurances that whatever the Tryleskian people needed, the crew could handle. The door to the office was already open, and Cathian was seated behind his desk. Raff and Dovis were there as well, but no one else.

He frowned at that. It seemed odd. The entire crew should be assembled to learn the details.

He seated Sara and stood behind her chair, crossing his arms. His friends looked angry for some reason. Raff had a deadly calm expression as he fingered the blade handles on his belt. Soft growls were rumbling from Dovis's chest.

He looked to Cathian for an explanation. "What's going on?"

Cathian glanced at Sara, and then back to him. "A Prince Azerba of the Dunng contacted the Vellar family to issue a complaint. In turn, Rex contacted me to issue orders. We're not following them."

York tried to remember any dealings with that race but came up blank. The Dunng were mostly a mining race. They owned a string of planets that produced crystals, which were popular with a lot of other races for making jewelry. Perhaps the Tryleskians had had an issue with them in the past, before he'd joined the crew. "What orders are we going to refuse?"

100

Sara stood and shot around the chair, almost knocking him over. She wrapped her arms around his waist, burying her face against his chest and clinging to him.

"It's the asshole who bought me to be a part of his harem! I remember the name."

Pure rage boiled through York as he held her tightly. His gaze shot to Cathian. "What did Rex say?"

"The prince contacted someone on Relon and was informed she was bonded to a crew member aboard our ship. Then the prince contacted my family. Rex ordered us to turn your female over to this prince...asshole. It's not happening. I explained that Sara was sold to the prince against her will, and that we aren't turning her over to become his slave. I reminded him that Tryleskians abhor slavery, and we never condone it. It's fine, Sara. We're not turning you over to anyone."

Sara didn't calm at Cathian's words.

"No one will take you from me," York swore, stroking Sara's back.

That did the trick. Her death grip on him eased a little and she looked up into his eyes. The tears and fear he saw nearly gutted him.

"I'd kill anyone who tried to take you from me," he swore. "No shoving them to the ground. There would be blood and death." He knew his voice had deepened. To talk of brutal violence might frighten her more, but he needed her to understand that he'd do whatever it took to keep her safe and with him.

His Sara gave him a watery smile. "You'd rip a prince apart for me?"

"Without hesitation. You're mine."

101

"I love you, York."

It was the first time she'd said it, and he couldn't stop his smile. "You have my heart as well." He met Cathian's intense gaze. "How angry is your family and the Tryleskians going to be over refusing their direct order? Do you think they will attempt to take *The Vorge* from us?"

"I don't care how angry they become or what they want to do," his friend replied. "We're not turning your female over to anyone. Nor are they getting our ship. Rex gave those assholes our location to meet up with us. He was certain we'd comply when he did so."

York flashed his fangs, a growl of rage rumbling from him.

Cathian nodded. "Rex is a fucking idiot. My father is, too, for believing I'd hand over one of my crew's bond mates. I'm hoping one day that they'll learn, but I doubt it. Remember the shit they tried to pull on *me* while I was going through my heat? I sure haven't."

"We'll change course," Dovis snarled. "Or blow the bastards up."

"Better yet, let them dock with us." Raff continued to fondle his blades. "I haven't killed in a while. It would be fun."

"I'm with Raff. What reason did Rex give as to why they'd even issue that order? Your people don't condone slavery." York tried to think through his rage. "Did you make it clear this prince bought her to be his sex slave? He already owns a harem of females, from what Sara learned."

Cathian tapped his desk, pulling up a document. "They are more than aware. Prince Azerba claims Sara is his property. He even sent *this* to my father. It's a bill of sale from Earth for your bond mate. His proof that Sara belongs to him." He tapped to display another document. It was a photo of Sara. "My father and his assistant are ignoring the law because Prince

102

Azerba runs Dais Two in the Dunng system. That's the mining planet a previous Tryleskian ambassador tried to negotiate with to get Piz crystals. Prince Azerba said he's open to talk trade if Sara is returned to him."

York flashed his fangs, even angrier. "They are willing to take my Sara for stones to put in *jewelry*?" He wanted to beat on something. No, *someone*. Cathian's father, to start. Rex next.

Sara turned to peer at Cathian. York eased his hold on her but kept her in the circle of his arms.

"The Relon who found me said they put out an arrest warrant for my buyer, in case he showed up on their planet attempting to get me. Doesn't that matter? He's a fugitive from the law."

York had forgotten about that in his anger. "That's right. You mentioned he was being sought for breaking Relon law." He glanced at his friends.

They smiled back. Cathian even laughed.

"What's funny?" Sara asked.

He looked down at his precious mate. "You're very smart."

"So it helps that he's wanted on Relon?"

York nodded. "Yes. Tryleskian has signed a multi-planet agreement and sworn to follow certain laws. Including not trading with criminals." He held Cathian's gaze. "Please tell me Relon is one of those planets, as well."

Cathian tapped his desk, getting the information. "I'm almost certain but let me verify." He grinned big as he lifted his head. "Yes."

"Let's invite the prince to come aboard *The Vorge*. Once he steps foot inside, it will be our duty to arrest him on behalf of Relon." Dovis sounded almost thrilled.

"That means I can't kill him." Raff sighed, but then his expression got slightly more animated. "Princes have guards. They'll attempt to stop us from taking him. I'll still get my fight."

"Don't kill anyone," Cathian ordered. "Unless you have no other choice." He was tapping for more information. A photo appeared over his desk. "Look at that. A wanted notice for one Prince Azerba. That's all we need."

Sara shivered in York's arms, and he pulled her close again. "Are you cold?"

She shook her head, tearing her gaze off the image hovering above Cathian's desk to stare up at him. "He's so gross-looking."

York studied the alien who'd have harmed his bond mate if he'd gotten ahold of her. She was correct. He was one unpleasant creature in appearance. Prince Azerba was a Dunng. They had greasy puffs of hair all over their bodies. Loose folds of skin hung off his arms and chin, where his clothing didn't cover. One large hump protruded from the male's back, giving him a slightly hunched frame.

"No wonder he has to buy females. Who'd willingly touch that? I bet every brothel he walks into turns him away, regardless of his expensive crystals. The workers would riot if the owners expected them to service that ugly beast." Raff paused. "At least they turn *me* down out of fear. That shaft-head is pure ugly."

104

York felt pity for any female slaves who hadn't been saved and ended up in the prince's harem. He stroked Sara's back again, reassuring her. "He won't get close to you, my heart. This I swear."

She hugged him, pressing her face to his chest again. "I trust you, baby."

"It's a privilege to protect you."

"It's a privilege for all of us to protect our females," Cathian corrected York.

"I just like to kill," Raff muttered. "Any reason will do."

York shot him a warning look. He didn't want Sara to think a member of their crew was a bit crazy and bloodthirsty.

Raff shrugged. "What? He's a slave buyer. Your female was bought and sold. You're not offended, are you, Sara?"

She shook her head. "No. Not at all. Now that I've seen what he looks like, I'll probably have nightmares about what he'd have done to me. None of it would have been good. I feel zero compassion for someone like that."

Once again, York felt pride. His bond mate was fierce.

"Let's get ready to receive our guests." Dovis grinned—then fur started to grow out of his skin and soft popping noises sounded as he began to shift forms. His nose pushed outward, along with his jaw.

York moved fast, blocking Sara's view of him and hustling her out of Cathian's office. He figured she'd been through enough already without seeing Dovis preparing to meet an enemy. His friend had purposely stayed in skin at York's request during their shared meal. He'd wanted Sara to get to know Dovis before she saw him in fur.

"Send an alert to let me know when they are within range." No way did York plan to miss a moment of the prince docking with *The Vorge*. He personally wanted to put the shaft-head in restraints and haul him into the cell they kept for prisoners.

Chapter Eight

Sara stood on the bridge with most of the crew. Another ship flew into view on a large vid screed, the one carrying her buyer. It wasn't nearly as big as the ship they were on.

York had wanted her locked inside their cabin, but she would have gone crazy not knowing what was going on. She'd asked that he take her somewhere safe, where she could still watch what happened. York, being a sweetheart, had agreed.

Cathian sat in the captain's chair. "Open comms."

York sat at a station, Sara hovering at his side. He'd insisted she stand where she'd be out of sight of the vid camera. His fingers flew over the console and live footage of the Dunng appeared where only the ship and space had been before.

A shudder ran down her spine when she saw Prince Azerba and at least five other aliens who looked just like him. Only their clothing was different, and she guessed her buyer was the one who wore a lot of jewelry. She also assumed the yellow stones embedded in every piece were the crystals he wanted to trade to get his hands on her.

York reached over to cup her thigh, his fingers wrapping around her leg. "I'd never let anyone take you from me, my heart," he whispered.

She forced a smile. "I know."

"Do you havzz my female ready to transsssport?"

The hissy voice sent more shivers down her spine. The prince sounded like a snake. It would have been horrible if she'd been delivered to him, if the Relon police hadn't saved her. She didn't even want to consider what kind of horrors she'd have faced.

"You must be Prince Azerba. I'm Ambassador Cathian Vellar. We do have the human. Come on over to get her."

"No. Sssend a transssport to my ssship."

"We can't do that," Cathian lied. "We didn't expect this to happen. Our shuttle is down for routine repairs. You're going to have come get her or wait a few days until the engine gets put back together."

The alien prince hissed and glared at Cathian. "I'll sssend my troopsss."

"Your what?" Cathian leaned forward in his chair. "That didn't translate."

"My men." Prince Azerba flashed rows of crooked, greenish teeth in what she guessed was irritation. "They getzzz my female."

Dovis stepped forward to stand behind Cathian. It had shocked Sara when she'd finally seen him in full fur. He really did resemble Earth's version of a werewolf, the horror movie kind that walked on two legs instead of four. His eyes were pitch black when he was in shift.

She glanced at the prince to see how he reacted to all that fur and the sharp claws. She was pretty sure that was fear she saw flashing on his saggy-skinned features.

"I'm Dovis, head of security and protocols." He made a slight bow. "I'm afraid you personally must sign for the human female. The Tryleskian officials have demanded proof that we've turned her over to you. We don't want any issues to arise. I believe you made a deal with them?"

108

"You did offer to open trade negotiations in exchange for the female," Cathian added. "A deal is a deal. You're welcome to bring some of your guards with you. Not that you'll need them. My planet is very interested in obtaining your crystals. Our females love to acquire rare and beautiful things."

Sara reached out and put her hand on York's shoulder, just wanting to hold on to him. Their plan hinged on getting the prince to board *The Vorge*. As she understood it, it would be considered an act of war if they breached the other ship to arrest him there. As much as she hated the alien who'd bought her, she didn't want to cause trouble for York and his crew.

Her bond mate reached up and placed his hand over hers, holding on to her tightly, too. It was reassuring.

The prince hissed loud and long. "I sssend my troopsss!"

"Not if you want the female," Dovis's voice deepened. "Protocols must be met. You need to sign for her yourself. Your men can't do that for you, Prince Azerba."

Another loud hiss came from the prince. "Fine. Ssshow me her first. Prove you havzzz."

York released her hand, giving her a slight nod.

Marrow came forward, a determined expression on her face. "Look scared," she whispered to Sara. "Arms behind your back to give them the impression you've been restrained. No talking."

Sara gave a sharp nod. They'd already talked about the possibility of the prince wanting eyes on her first. She locked her fingers together at her spine and walked toward Cathian to be in view of the screen. Marrow stayed right behind her, looking intimidating in her black uniform.

Marrow put one hand on her shoulder and brought them both to stop.

"Here's the Earth woman," Marrow announced. "She's cuffed and ready for you to pick her up, your highness."

Sara couldn't stare at the prince for long. She felt sick when he approached the screen, his face becoming huge. He had small sores in the creases of the skin rolls on his face. She thought they might be pimples. She wasn't sure, but whatever they were, they matched his green teeth. It disgusted her enough to glance at the floor.

"I ssshall enjoy you. We come now."

The screen returned to the view of space and the other ship.

Marrow released her shoulder. "That is one putrid male. Is he diseased?"

"Everyone grab a pair of gloves on our way to greet the shaft-head," Cathian ordered. "Let's not risk it."

"Extending the docking sleeve," York growled, sounding furious. "Their transport is on the way. I'm going to enjoy getting my hands on that asshole."

"Wear gloves," Sara reminded him. "Please."

York stood, walking over to her. "Don't worry. Stay here with Marrow. She'll activate the security feeds that will allow you to watch everything that happens." He addressed Marrow next. "Be prepared to undock with their transport and get us out of here once we have the prince onboard. Raise shields right away. They'll probably fire on us, trying to take out our engines. I would."

"I give the orders," Cathian reminded York, pausing next to them. Then he smirked. "Do what York said. Dovis has already set course for Relon. You just need to get us away from their ship once we have our prisoner, Marrow. We're going to drop that trash off as soon as we collect it. And seal the doors after us, just in case one of them breaks away and tries to get to the bridge. They don't look like fighters, but I always prefer to be prepared. Everyone else is in lockdown until this ends."

"You got it, Captain." Marrow walked to York's station, taking his seat.

York leaned down and brushed his lips over Sara's. "It's going to be fine. Trust me."

"I do. Kick ass, baby."

He grinned. "I appreciate that you aren't afraid when I have to resort to beating on idiots."

"Just don't lose. That's all I ask."

"Never."

She watched him, Cathian, and Dovis leave. The doors sealed, and she knew Marrow had immediately locked them. The other crew had decided to stay inside their cabins. The Pods were monitoring thoughts from the other ship, staying in telepathic communication with York and the other two men with him.

"No worries, Sara." Marrow got up and took the captain's chair. "We've been in worse situations than this over the years. This should be easy. Ready to track the crew?"

Sara turned, watching as the main screen split into various views of the ship. The feeds followed the men, showing them from different angles as they left the lift and walked down the corridors. She saw they open a compartment and put on gloves.

"The transport is docking now."

"Thanks for telling me."

Marrow chuckled. "I was telling *them*."

York, Dovis, and Cathian stopped near where the docking sleeve was located. Sara remembered it from when she'd boarded with York. Raff approached them from behind, wearing all black and strapped with at least two dozen knives and daggers.

Sara gasped.

"Didn't York tell you that Raff grew up to become a feared assassin? He loves sharp shit, can hit anything he aims at, and he's got two guns inside his boots. Also, never pat him on the back when he's dressed like that and geared up for battle. The crazy bastard has a longer blade strapped down his spine and it's got a bomb that's part of the handle."

Sara was dumbfounded. "Um, isn't that dangerous on a ship? Bombs mean depressurization and stuff."

"It's only there for emergencies. I wasn't lying about how Raff always hits what he's aiming for. It's not a big bomb, and only he can activate it. He sometimes practices inside cargo hold two when it's empty. The explosives aren't large enough to even dent the floor but his target still blows up."

That didn't make Sara feel any better. York was just feet away from the assassin. She didn't want him in blast range.

She realized exactly how much she loved him already...how much she didn't want to live her life without him...and her hand flattened on her stomach.

She wanted to have a little York baby. He was willing to protect her with his life. She'd be proud to bear his children. The more time she spent thinking about getting pregnant, the more appealing it sounded.

Marrow pointed at the screen. "Oh good. All of them put on gloves. I was worried Raff would ignore that order. I don't want whatever it is those aliens have to spread through the crew. Our medical android is great but remind me to tell you sometime about the Gorin spores we encountered on a mission. We were all exposed and sporting red rashes for three days until the cure kicked in. It was so bad, we were all working naked. It hurt to wear clothing!"

Sara really didn't want to hear that story.

* * * * *

York kept his anger off his face. They all did. Cathian stood slightly in front of him, with Dovis at the captain's side. Raff hung back, trying to stay mostly out of sight. He tended to make anyone who saw him nervous and afraid. They needed the prince to step foot on *The Vorge* to make the arrest legal.

113

The docking doors slid open and two guards entered first, followed by the shaft-head who wanted to take his Sara away. Instinct had York's hands clenching, wanting to rip the pompous prince to pieces. Lots of them. The ugly alien had bought his beautiful Sara and had come thinking he could take her away and use her. That alone was reason for the alien to die a grisly, painful death.

Cathian played his ambassador role well, giving a slight nod of his head. "Welcome to *The Vorge*. We're honored to have you, Prince Azerba. Please be our guest for a few drinks."

"No. Givzzz the female now."

"Of course. Follow me. She's in a holding cell just down this corridor. I have the transfer papers all ready for you to sign." Cathian turned, giving the three his back.

Dovis stepped aside, prepared to protect their captain in case one of the guards attacked.

The Dunng guards hesitated, glancing at their prince for orders. York wondered nervously if he'd decide not to risk getting on the ship after all.

He breathed a silent sigh of relief when the prince hissed and stepped out of the sleeve and onto *The Vorge*. His guards remained in front of him, following Cathian.

The moment they were clear of the docking doors, they auto-closed.

Startled, the guards and the prince spun around. "Whatzzz the meaning of thisss?"

Dovis stepped closer to the Dunng. "Prince Azerba, you are under arrest. We're taking you to Relon. They've issued a warrant for your

114

capture. As representatives for the law-abiding Tryleskian leaders, we're not going to harbor a wanted criminal on our vessel. Under the Treaty of Multiple Planets, clause 163 under legal rights and responsibilities, it's my duty to turn you over to Relon authorities."

The floor under them vibrated, and York braced himself a second before the entire vessel jerked slightly. The motion normally wasn't that pronounced when they went from a dead stop to engaging the engines, but Marrow needed to get them underway fast, before the Dunng ship realized they'd just taken their boarding party and cut the docking sleeve connection to their shuttle.

The guards attacked.

York was ready to fight but Raff and Dovis had them pinned on the ground in seconds. It was almost sad how quickly they were subdued. He'd been looking forward to a good fight.

The prince hissed louder and fumbled with his clothing, probably reaching for a hidden weapon.

York lunged, grabbed his arm and jerked it back, hearing bone break. A high-pitched keening erupted from the prince. York grabbed him under his sagging chins next, wrapping his gloved hand around the bastard's throat. It was tempting to crush it—but he refrained.

"Sara is *mine*," he snarled. "*My* bond mate. Did you think I'd just hand her over to you? That I'd allow you to sexually abuse her? Keep her in a cage? Locked up and miserable?" He lifted the smaller alien off his feet, slamming him against the wall.

"York," Cathian warned. "Don't kill him. I know everything inside is urging you to do so, but drop him. Please. We have a plan, remember? Stick to it."

York struggled with the decision, his rage that great, but logic won. He released the prince. Raff was there the second he backed off, searching the alien and taking two weapons he found stashed inside the prince's clothing.

"You're a sad, sorry race," Raff muttered to the Dunng. "That takedown was disappointing. I didn't even have to kill anyone."

York glared at the prince, still wanting to rip him apart.

Cathian gripped York's shoulder. "I understand wanting to make him stop breathing so he'll never be a threat to your human again. I do. But the Relons aren't lenient on slave owners. And we don't want to start a war with the Dunng."

"You havzzz!" the prince yelled. "We will kill youzzz all!"

"Shut up. Take him to a cell, Raff. Dovis, put his guards in an escape pod and launch them off our vessel before we get too far from their ship." Cathian released York's shoulder. "Return to Sara. Hold her. It will make you feel calmer. We've got this from here. I'm going to conveniently ignore any incoming comms from his people *and* my own until we reach Relon and hand the prince over to their authorities. Then I'll deal with my displeased father and his annoying assistant."

York turned to his friend after Dovis and Raff dragged the Dunng guards away. "How much trouble are you going to be in? Tell me the truth."

Cathian blinked a few times. "We're doing the legally correct thing. I'll remind Rex of that, *and* my father. I kept the recordings of our conversations, including the one shortly before the Dunng ship arrived, where I made it clear Prince Azerba bought a human slave and had a warrant issued for his arrest—and they gave me orders to turn her over regardless. You know the Vellars will do anything to avoid a scandal. I'll threaten to release those recordings to the public if they try to strip me of my duties or even threaten to take *The Vorge* from us. It would tarnish our family name if it was linked in any way to helping a slaver." Cathian's voice lowered. "We also have Raff."

York nodded. "They certainly don't want *him* causing trouble."

"No, they do not. It's obvious he's a Vellar. That would create questions no one wants to answer—like who his father is and why he wasn't raised by my uncle. I've made it clear that Raff will be returning home with me if they force us back. They'll want to keep all of us out here in space more than they'll want to punish the crew for losing some overpriced crystals."

"Thank you." York felt immense gratitude toward Cathian for going against his orders from his home planet to keep Sara safe.

"There's no need for those words ever to pass your lips, my friend. Your Sara is one of us now. Family protects each other."

York nodded. "We do."

"Go to her. You'll feel better once she's in your arms. Nara always eases my anger."

He left Cathian and tore off his gloves, even the uniform top, before reaching the bridge. He didn't want any part of the clothing that had touched the vile prince to taint her soft skin.

The door had been locked, as ordered, but it opened quickly. Marrow would have seen him on the security feeds.

He'd barely stepped inside when Sara launched herself at him. He opened his arms, caught her, and lifted her against his taller frame. He buried his face between her neck and shoulder, inhaling her scent.

"It's over. We have the prince in custody, Sara."

"I know. I saw it all go down." She clung to him, her arms wrapped around his neck. "Thank you."

"Hey," Marrow called out. "Look at the vid screen." She chuckled. "Seems Prince Shaft-head doesn't like being locked inside a cell."

York slowly lowered Sara and lifted his head, peering at the screen. There was a security feed displaying Prince Azerba yanking on the bars of the cell, his mouth open wide, showing off his green teeth. He appeared to be yelling but the sound wasn't on.

He smiled as the Dunng royalty spun and threw himself on the floor, kicking and pounding it with his fists.

"He's acting like a big two-year-old," Sara said. "He's actually throwing a temper tantrum!"

"Is that what it is?" Marrow smirked. "I was about to send the medical android to check on him."

"You probably should do that anyway to make certain those green sores aren't contagious." York reached up and cupped Sara's face, holding her gaze.

"On it," Marrow muttered. "I'm very glad I'm a shuttle pilot and not a doctor. You couldn't pay me enough to examine that ugly beast up close."

"I'm very glad this is as close as I'll ever get to him," Sara admitted, laughing.

"It's good to see you laugh." York caressed his bond mate.

"I can't believe I was so terrified of that thing." She glanced back at the screen and chuckled. "He's rolled over, and now he's crying. I guess he doesn't enjoy being held against his will, under the control of someone else. Serves him right."

York still wanted to kill the Dunng prince, but he let it go. "We should return to our cabin. I still have a few days off." He turned his focus to Marrow. "That is, if you don't need help. Status?"

"The Dunng ship slowed briefly and picked up the emergency pod, probably hoping their sniveling prince was inside with the two guards. They've obviously figured out we've got him, since they're now coming after us. We're ignoring their comm hails."

"They're following?" York wasn't surprised but he didn't like it, either.

Marrow turned in her seat. "I've got this. I increased speed. They aren't going to be able to catch us. Their engines are less powerful. We'll have time to transport his royal ugliness to the surface of Relon before they hit the planet's orbit."

119

York wanted to be certain the Relon authorities charged the alien for buying Sara. "Let me know when we reach the planet."

Marrow shook her head. "Don't worry about who's taking him down. The shaft-head sent enough proof to the Tryleskians to establish his guilt. Including an image of his purchase." Her gaze darted to Sara before returning to him. "He's convicted himself. Raff has offered to tag along. I'll fly the larger shuttle to the surface and he'll pull guard duty. Dovis is also going, to fill out the legal documents, since he's officially our head of security. We've got this. Go bond."

York didn't need to be told twice. He grabbed Sara's hand and led her off the bridge. "You're always safe, Sara. Never forget that."

"I won't."

They reached their cabin within minutes and York lifted her into his arms the second the door sealed behind them. He kissed her, carrying her to their bed. The overriding urge to plant his seed inside her and watch her belly expand in size with his young had his shaft swollen and hurting. He gently put her down, bending to remove his boots.

Sara stripped fast, too. "God, you are so sexy."

"So are you, my heart."

He removed the last of his clothing, reaching for his bond mate.

There was an urgency to their lovemaking. He explored her body feverishly with his hands and mouth, loving the tiny moans she made, and the way she touched him back. He kissed her deep when she was wet and ready for him, her thighs parting to wrap around his hips, and he surged forward, claiming her.

Pleasure had him groaning her name as he furiously pumped his hips, her sounds of pending climax growing louder when he increased the pace.

He hoped when his seed expelled from his shaft, that it would result in a child. Fate had blessed them once already. He was hopeful for a second time.

Chapter Nine

Sara couldn't believe she was already back on Relon. The authorities had asked that she appear before one of their judging committees as proof she was the human Prince Azerba had illegally purchased. It seemed the Dunng were trying to state their prince had been set up, a tactic by the Tryleskians in order to gain Piz crystals.

York kept making angry noises at her side, and he tightened his hold on her hand. "They have no honor!"

"It's bullshit," Sara agreed. "But we've got this."

York was upset, and she didn't blame him. He hadn't wanted her to go down to the planet surface, certain the Dunng meant to attack or outright kill her before she could arrive in court.

She glanced at their party. York, Marrow, Raff, Cathian, and one of the Pods were with her. She felt safe.

"It's going to be fine, York. You heard Cathian. The Dunng believe my race is weak and too frightened to face their prince in court. They're hoping I won't show, so they can get the charges dismissed to free him."

"Exactly," Cathian agreed. "These idiots have no idea how strong and determined humans can be. Nara wanted to come with us but I talked her into helping Dovis defend *The Vorge* while we're down here. They might try to attack it after their prince is found guilty."

"It feels like a trap," York muttered.

"I'm certain it is." Raff almost sounded excited. "When shit goes bad, Marrow can shield One. York, you're on Sara. I'll kill anything that comes at us from the front and sides, while Cathian will cover our asses. They might slow us down, but we'll make it to court on time."

Sara glanced at Raff. He actually looked happy for once. She was glad he was on their side. York, however, still appeared grim, his gaze taking in everything around them, ready to protect her if they were attacked. She trusted him.

The street outside the transport shuttle was congested with aliens. Most saw their group and scattered, making a wide path. York pulled her closer to his side. One walked next to Sara, with Marrow on his other side. Raff stayed ahead of them, with Cathian at their backs. It left One and Sara completely surrounded.

A small hand brushed hers, and she startled before grasping One's hand. A sense of calm filled her, and she wondered if pushing emotions into others was one of the Pod's gifts, besides reading minds. It seemed he was trying to let her know everything would be okay.

"Everything *will* be fine, and yes, we can," One said quietly, in response to her thoughts. "Captain, two minds are focused on us," he warned. "They are Yuna, who are working for the Dunng. The first is surprised we showed, the other is frustrated Sara didn't come with just one guard. He's under orders to grab her and take her to a waiting Dunng ship. He now realizes that's not possible." He paused—then giggled. "He's afraid of York. He saw a Parri male in a jealous rage once, when one of the Yuna's friends made the mistake of groping the breast of a Parri female in the market, to see if it was as soft as it looked. His friend didn't survive."

Sara had a mental flashback of the shelter instructor showing her the result of a Parri attack. She wondered if that alien's friend had been the same dead Yuna in the picture, the one who'd been torn to pieces. Despite the grisly reminder, her fear faded. York could definitely fight. She trusted his friends to keep her safe, too.

It had confused her at first, why One had come with them, but now she understood. He was the perfect detection system if anyone meant to attack.

"I'm good at it, too," One boasted. "Captain, we're being followed by the first one. They want her alive to return to the prince, but they're allowed to kill her if capture isn't possible. He's in communication with two groups, letting them know when to attack. They didn't want a public street fight but are under orders to not let the human reach court."

"Yes!"

Sara startled from Raff's outburst before he glanced back at their group. A wide grin stretched his lips and sheer excitement glowed on his features. He faced forward again, his hands fondling the blade handles at his hips.

York urged her to keep walking. "He gets unnaturally thrilled about fighting. Try to ignore it."

Marrow snorted. "Is your shaft hard, Raff? Most males get turned on by a naked woman, but not you."

"The condition of my shaft is never any of your business," Raff grunted.

"We have incoming," One announced. "There are too many minds to get an accurate count but it's in the dozens. They are in front of us and to the left." He paused. "They have an echo launcher!"

York released Sara's hand, grabbed her around her waist, and swiftly jerked her off her feet.

She gasped, seeing that Marrow had done the same to One. York ran to a public communication box and shoved her inside.

"Get down and stay there!"

She'd barely sat when One was dropped on top of her in the enclosed space. It was a good thing he didn't weigh much. The box reminded her of Earth's version of an old telephone booth. One wiggled a bit, getting off her lap and pressing against her side, and Sara drew her legs up, making herself a smaller target. They were squeezed together tightly, with York in front of them, blocking the opening.

"We'll be fine." One patted her hand. "No one will reach us."

"What's an echo launcher?"

"It projects strong wind," he whispered.

"That doesn't sound too bad." She'd been afraid they'd launch bombs or toxic gas that would kill everyone.

One gasped, then yelled, "Launching!"

York suddenly turned, grabbed the small counter above them, and curved his body over theirs.

A loud blast hit, hurting Sara's ears.

She could see between York's slightly parted legs in front of them. There was a store about fifteen feet away—and the glass in the front shattered inward and people inside were thrown off their feet, towards the back of the store. All the merchandise on the shelves inside went flying, too. It reminded Sara of a shockwave effect.

Her ears rang from the noise, and the box they were in shook but held firm.

York shoved himself back, gone in a flash. He moved out of their sight, and Sara tried to leave the box to go help, but One clutched at her. She turned her head, seeing his lips moving, but she couldn't hear what he said. He tightened his hold and jerked on her, forcing her to stay put. It took seconds for the ringing in her ears to fade.

"I said," One repeated, "stay down! We'll only be in their way. Neither of us are fighters."

That's where he was wrong. Sara heard grunts, the sound of a vicious fight, then laser blasts going off. She stared at the sidewalk between her hiding spot and the store. The urge to fight at York's side was strong.

"Don't," One warned. "You're thinking as a human. I'm sure you're strong, but not against a Yuna. Be smart. Not proud. You're no match for aliens bigger and faster than you. You'll become a distraction to the crew that could get them killed."

She grit her teeth. The truth hurt. Everything inside her hated taking cover while the crew risked their lives for her safety.

"I know you find this difficult," One whispered. "Stay put, Sara. I need to focus. Let me do my job. Yours is staying right here."

She nodded. "Okay." She hoped the crew didn't get hurt or killed, not sure how she'd be able to live with the guilt.

One chuckled. "They're all fine. Feel sorry for the Yuna. They're dying swiftly. Raff isn't holding back. Neither are the others. Stop feeling guilt, as well; none of this was your doing. Blame the Dunng prince. He's the one who hired these thugs to attack us."

Something shrieked. It was close and sounded horrible. Green liquid splashed the sidewalk in front of the box.

"Incoming Relon police," One shouted. "They're on our side. Don't kill them, too."

Sara glanced at him with an incredulous look.

One met her gaze. "The crew needs to know who the enemy is. We've had experiences in the past with officials who were bribed. The Relon are here to assist."

"Ah...okay."

It grew quiet after a few more minutes. One wiggled his fingers, finally motioning her to get out of the box. "It's safe. All are down but our crew."

She gripped the sides of the opening and pulled herself out.

The first thing she saw when she stood were bodies. A lot of them.

York faced her from a few feet away. He had green stuff all over him—but what scared her most was the red blood smeared over one of his cheeks.

"I'm fine, my Sara. It's just a scratch. I heal fast."

"Help me, please."

Sara had forgotten about One. He struggled to get up but his round little body was kind of stuck. She took both his hands and pulled him to his feet.

"I told you it would be fine." He winked. "It's always best for everyone if we stay out of the way while they fight."

She released him and wanted to rush to York, but he shook his head, putting out a hand to stop her. "I don't want their blood on you."

"Right." Her gaze went to his cheek again. "Are you sure you're okay?"

"I would never lie to you."

She nodded, then looked around, finding Marrow. The pilot was wiping her face and hands with what looked to be someone's torn shirt. Raff walked among the downed Yunas, pulling blades from their bodies and returning them to various holsters on his pants. Cathian motioned to the group of Relon police and began to talk to them. They were too far away for Sara to hear what was being said.

She counted over twenty-six Yuna on the ground. All the other aliens who'd been in the street before the fight broke out were slowly stepping out of shops with damaged windows. They must have rushed inside them when the fight broke out. No innocent bystanders appeared gravely injured, but some were sporting cuts and torn clothing from the launcher damage.

Those people looked as stunned as Sara felt at seeing the destruction and bodies.

Her crew had taken on all those Yuna—and won. Not only that, but none of the Yuna were moving. She was pretty sure all twenty-six were dead. A few of the Yuna attackers near York were in pieces. She quickly averted her gaze, though that didn't come as a shock. Nor did it make her fear York, who she was certain had done that damage.

"It's going to be fine," York assured her.

She forced a smile. "I know. Thank you. This is my first, um, battle. I'm so proud of you...but I'm a little grossed out. Not from you. It's the bodies."

York's expression softened. "I'd do anything to keep you safe."

"I love you."

"You're my heart. I want to hold you, but..." He motioned down his body.

"After a shower," she agreed.

He chuckled. "Yes."

"Let's go, crew," Cathian ordered. "We'll be late for court. The Relons are going to make sure we're not attacked again." He glanced around. "And they'll take care of this mess by clearing away the bodies."

"I told you these idiots would only slow us down." Raff chuckled. "That was fun, wasn't it?"

"I have blood in my hair," Marrow growled. "Gross."

"I didn't send any heads your way this time," York told her. "You're welcome."

Sara frowned, glancing between the two, wondering what that meant.

"You don't want to know," One sighed, taking Sara's hand. "You heard the captain. We need to go. Court awaits. Let's make the asshole prince pay for his crimes."

York walked next to Sara but was careful not to brush up against her. She reached out and gripped his pinkie finger. It was the only part of his hand not stained green.

Their group took formation again, with her and One in the center. But now they had armed Relon escorts, too.

"That's their justice hall." York used his free hand to point at a building. "We made it."

"It's all good, Captain," One stated. "I have no more thoughts from anyone about attacking us. The prince has already learned we took out his hired thugs and Sara is alive." He paused, then giggled again. "He's aware he's going to be convicted—and has just burst into tears."

* * * * *

Court was long and boring, but Sara patiently listened to the judges drone on about the charges and the evidence. As for her part, she just needed to be there for the prosecutor to point out. She hadn't had to testify at all. Her presence alone proved she was real. And then it finally got to the good part

A Relon guard ordered Prince Azerba to his feet to face punishment. Not only did he have to pay for the damage his thugs had caused on the street when they'd attacked *The Vorge* crew, but he was sentenced to fifty years in prison.

One of the judges lifted a hand. "We will remove one year each for the safe return of any slaves you've purchased, your highness."

"But you *will* serve at least twenty years," another added. "I hope you have thirty slaves to relinquish. Otherwise, I doubt you'll see your home world again. You'll die in the bowels of Relon."

Sara was surprised by the court's offer, but she hoped the prince took them up on it and freed his harem. Twenty years was a long time, regardless. She wouldn't have to worry about him seeking payback for two decades or more.

The prince sobbed and threw himself on the floor, kicking and screaming as he had on *The Vorge*. "Do you know who I am? I'm a prince! You can't do this to me!"

One of the judges snorted. "You own mines. Now you'll work in one. We find that a fitting punishment."

York leaned in, whispering to her, "The prison they speak of is a mining operation a few thousand feet underground. There's no hope of escape or a prison break. I've heard the few shafts leading to it are rigged to blow if they're ever breached by anyone unauthorized. He'd be buried alive if that were to happen. It's a failsafe. They send the worst criminals underground. I'm glad he'll be sent there instead of a surface camp. They probably fear his people would attempt to rescue him."

That information comforted her even more.

The session broke up and the condemned had to be carried out by two guards, the prince still screaming and wailing. Sara didn't feel sympathy for him. He'd not only bought her to be his sex slave, but had tried to take her from York. Other victims of his probably hadn't been as lucky or had anyone to protect them.

"It's finished. He'll never dare to come after you again." York looked pleased.

"His family might," Raff retorted.

"Don't even think it." Cathian glared at his cousin. "You're always looking for a fight." He met Sara's gaze. "The prince's family will be more

131

focused on trying to get that prick out of prison and attempting to make shady deals to cut off more years."

"Is that possible?"

Cathian shook his head. "Relons are honorable. They abhor slavery. It's at the top of a list of crimes they allow no forgiveness for. It will take a while for his family to figure that out, though."

"I'm ready to fly us back home." Marrow led the way out of the building.

"Should we stop to get cleaned up first?" York had the most blood on him.

"No. All the blood has dried by now. We won't be staining our shuttle seats, and I'll feel better once we're off the surface. No sense in sticking around any longer than necessary." Cathian pulled out a comms unit. "I'm letting Nara and the rest of the crew know what went down and that we're on our way back."

Another Relon escort team met them in the street and walked them all the way back to their shuttle. They probably wanted to avoid another attack and more damage to their city. York helped her get buckled into a seat and then excused himself, rushing into the bathroom. She smiled, knowing he wanted to get as clean as possible.

Marrow started the engines and they lifted off. York returned to his seat minus his shirt, his skin and hair wet, and she got a better look at his injured cheek, now that his blood had been washed away. He was right; it was just a thin scratch that looked mostly healed. She was thankful he had that ability. Humans would have taken more than just a few hours for an injury to fade.

He gave her a kiss on her lips. "I'm glad that's over."

"Me too." She looked at their group. "I want to tell everyone how much I appreciate the support you've given me."

Cathian turned in the copilot seat and smiled. "Just another day in the life we live. It rarely gets boring."

"I wouldn't say that." York lifted her hand and kissed it, then grinned at Cathian. "It was extremely boring before Sara came into my life. You were just too occupied with Nara to notice all the down time."

Chapter Ten

Sara woke to York kissing her shoulder. She lay on her stomach, her naked body stretched out on the bed. A smile curved her lips. They'd arrived back on *The Vorge* and basically locked themselves in their cabin. He'd showered, and then made love to her half a dozen times until they'd fallen asleep.

"Good morning."

"It is," he chuckled. "I love waking up with you."

She rolled, reaching for him, and brushed her lips over his. "And I love sleeping with you."

"I love how adorable you are while you sleep. You pet me."

"I do?" That surprised her.

"Yes." He nodded. "Your hands roam my body. It feels wonderful." He paused, frowning. "Let's go have breakfast. Your stomach is rumbling."

It was. They'd had a snack for dinner but not much more the evening before, not in the mood to mingle with the crew in the dining hall. That would have meant getting out of bed and putting on clothing. She rolled over and stood, wincing.

"That's another reason we're not staying in bed all day." York backed up toward the shower. "You're sore."

"You're big." She followed him. "I'm not complaining one bit about that, though."

He chuckled. "Go shower. I'll get our clothing."

"You're not going to join me?" She pushed out her lower lip, giving him a pout.

"Don't do that, bond mate. I'm on to you."

She laughed. "Yeah. Okay. But I like to see you wet."

"I can say the same for you, but you need to be fed. It's my duty to make sure you're taken care of. Priorities, bond mate. Food. Then we'll return here and I'll give you a massage."

She halted, staring up at him. "Seriously?"

"I love to touch you."

"Alright. Then I'm about to break speed records on showering and eating." She rounded him and entered the bathroom, turning on the water.

The sound of his laughter made her grin as she stood under the hot water.

Sara's thoughts turned to her previous life, comparing it to the one she had now. It amazed her how happy she felt. Earth had always been a struggle. To pay rent, to keep her job despite crappy bosses, to have enough money left over to eat. Now, she was about to enjoy a big meal, spend time with the huge blue man she'd fallen in love with, and looking forward to a massage from his talented hands.

She finished washing her hair right as York entered the stall. The sight of his muscled, amazing body would never get old. She reached out to stroke his abs but he jerked back, laughing.

"No. Food, massage, and then sex." He licked his lips. "Though I love your taste more."

"You're teasing, and that's just mean."

"Never, my Sara. It's a promise of what I plan to do later. Remember, priorities. My turn to get clean. Out!"

She *was* a bit sore. The guy had a big, thick cock, and she wasn't exactly used to marathon sex. But in time, she was pretty sure she would be—and that sounded fantastic.

She exited the shower, dried, and then brushed her teeth. He joined her when she was getting dressed and they left the cabin a few minutes later.

Some of the crew were missing when they entered the dining hall. York explained they were on duty. Dovis had the bridge, Mari was doing a repair, and Marrow was cleaning out the shuttle they'd used to go to Relon.

York steered her toward a table where the captain and Nara sat with the Pods. Sara dug into her meal, enjoying the chance to spend some time with her new friends.

She was nearly finished eating when all three Pods suddenly stood up.

"Raff, come with us. Captain, we're needed on the bridge," One said.

"Shit," Cathian muttered. "Who's approaching *now*?"

"No one. Dovis sent a mental message that Rex and your father have commed," Two answered. "They are demanding to speak with you immediately."

"They're going to pull some shit," Three grumbled. "At least Dovis thinks so."

Sara lost her appetite. She knew that Cathian's father was also his boss, and that he'd gone against orders by not turning her over to the prince.

York saw her alarmed expression and stood, too. "We'll go."

The captain turned at the door. "We've got this. Enjoy your meal." He glanced at Sara and smiled. "It's going to be fine."

Raff paused next to him. "Let the fun begin. I love messing with those assholes."

They left. Midgel got up and returned to the kitchen.

Nara hesitated only seconds before smiling and rushing after the group heading for the bridge. "They *do* have this, but I get so turned on watching my life-lock give hell to his asshole father and that piece-of-shit assistant of his!"

That left Sara and York alone in the dining hall. He lifted her hand, kissing it. "Don't look so frightened."

"What if they fire Cathian and all the crew? I know *The Vorge* belongs to the Tryleskian people. Doesn't his father pretty much run things there? We could lose our home."

York released her hand, grabbed her, and placed her on his lap. "That will never happen. Let me tell you a secret."

She wrapped her arms around his neck, peering into his beautiful blue eyes. "Will it make me feel better?"

"It will. We get into trouble *all* the time. It would shock Beltsen Vellar if his son actually complied with his every order. And I already told you about Raff. He's an effective deterrent for Cathian's father. Stop worrying, Sara."

"They fled out of here fast, though, as if it was urgent."

"I'm sure their haste wasn't out of fear. It was anger on Cathian's part. The rest just enjoy watching the show. You haven't met Beltsen or Rex. When you do, you'll understand what shaft-heads both males are. It's rather enjoyable to watch when they get taken to task."

She let that sink in. "You're sure things will work out?"

He nodded, his expression sincere. "Absolutely. What *should* be consuming your thoughts are our plans after breakfast. I'm finished eating. Are you?"

"Yes."

He adjusted his hold on her, lifting her into his arms as he stood. "We're still on our honeymoon. Are you ready for that massage?"

"That sounds perfect."

"*You're* perfect, my Sara. I love you."

"I love you, too, York. I feel so blessed to have found you. And very grateful that Nodo was such a bitch." She grinned.

He laughed, carrying her toward their cabin. "I'm relieved you saved me from her. Let's forget about Nagway."

"Yeah. We should focus on making babies instead."

He halted, locking his gaze to hers.

"I figure with the way we can't keep our hands off each other, the fact that I'm not on any form of birth control, *and* with your body changes, we're so going to get pregnant soon."

"Babies would be amazing! We'll have the cutest Parri-and-human-mix children of them all! I'll post their pictures just to make the other parents feel envy." He began to walk again, his strides faster than before. "We should have at least a dozen."

She laughed. "Let's try one or two and see how we do with them first."

"Whatever makes you happy."

"I already am."

* * * * *

Raff stood to the side, out of video range, as Cathian took the captain's chair and the vid screen connected their ship to the Tryleskian home world. Beltsen Vellar's face came into view.

Raff reached down, unconsciously fondling one of the blades strapped to his hip.

He held a grudge against his uncle, but he tried to let it go. Cathian had saved his life and given him a future the day he'd learned of Raff's existence. He'd flown *The Vorge* to Gluttren Four, the shit planet Raff had been raised on, taking him from there.

It would only cause problems if he killed Cathian's father.

"How dare you!" Beltsen hissed. "You turned the prince over to the Relons and ruined a perfect business opportunity for us. Our family would have made a fortune in profit!"

Cathian rose to his feet. "How dare *you*. That Dunng was a slaver, a piece of shit, and no amount of crystals are worth ruining our family name! Think on that."

Rex, Beltsen's assistant, made an appearance behind him. "No one would have found out."

"Wrong. I would have told everyone." Cathian sat back down. "I don't know why I expect either of you to have any integrity. Both of you disappoint me."

"One female wasn't worth the loss of profits." Beltsen's face turned red as he snarled, "I know you value humans, but no one else does. Their planet is barbaric, and now word is spreading that they're selling their own people. The Vax contacted me to see if we wanted to purchase females from Earth. They have an arrangement with the humans' government."

Cathian gripped the chair hard enough for the metal arms to creak in protest. "You'd better have refused."

"Of course I did," his father spat. "We don't deal in slaves here, and I certainly don't want more of our people *contaminated* the way you've been by your sex worker."

"Nara," Cathian snarled. "You'll address my life-lock properly. She was *not* a sex worker."

"She was bought, wasn't she?" Rex sneered. "To feed you during your heat. It was either that or prison for her, wasn't it? For smuggling drugs?"

"That's right." Beltsen smirked. "Stop threatening me, son. You have no room to talk about integrity and shaming the family name. You whisper a hint of scandal to the public, and I will do the same. *No one* would accept a sex worker into high society on our world. Never mind that she's human and beneath a Tryleskian of your standing. She'd be shunned by everyone."

Raff knew his cousin was about to lose his temper. Not that he'd blame Cathian if he wanted to plot a course to the planet to personally beat the hell out of both males. That would get him arrested, though. It was one thing to play mental games, but another to blatantly air their grievances for all to see.

He strode into range of the viewing screen, knowing both males would see him. He stopped behind Cathian and gripped his cousin's shoulder, giving it a firm squeeze in warning. Cathian glanced at him, his features a barely concealed mask of rage. He gave a sharp nod and sealed his lips together. Raff released him.

Beltsen's look was one of disgust. "And I'm getting tired of you using *him* as a threat, Cathian."

Raff looked up, holding the man's gaze. "He's not the one you have to worry about, Uncle."

Beltsen flinched.

"You see, Cathian is much nicer than I am. He warned you how bad it would be if anyone were to learn your brother got a female pregnant, knew about it, but abandoned her and his child on an uncivilized planet. It would ruin your family's precious good name." He moved around the chair, standing next to his cousin. "Do you know what my life was like?"

Beltsen waved as if unconcerned. "I read the report Cathian sent."

"Then you know what I'm capable of. I had to kill to stay alive. I was the only Tryleskian on the planet, taller and more muscular than anyone else. Every thug tried to force me into service for them. But I'll never be a slave to anyone. Life was difficult at best...and my mother was murdered. I hold you *and* your brother responsible for her death. She would be alive if you both hadn't abandoned her while pregnant."

Beltsen began to shake his head. "That's not my fault."

"You personally rescued your brother after his ship crashed on Gluttren Four, covered up the fact that he'd gone into heat and got my mother pregnant. She was three months along the day your shuttle landed. Don't lie. You should have taken my mother home with you. Given her a good life. She bore a Vellar male for your family!"

His uncle glared at him. "There was no verification of that. For all I knew, she was pregnant by another male."

"Lies—and any medical scan would have revealed I was a Vellar."

"It's plausible." A cunning expression tightened Beltsen's features.

Raff suddenly displayed a blade to the screen. "There's an interesting story about this weapon that you'll want to hear."

"I don't care," his uncle snapped.

Raff gave him a cold smile. "My mother sent out messages to the Vellar family when I was five years old. She didn't think she could keep me alive much longer, and she pleaded for help. Imagine her relief when two Tryleskians arrived a few weeks later, looking for us. They said that *you'd* sent them, Uncle Beltsen. They told us to pack. We were being saved."

Sweat broke out on his uncle's forehead and his eyes narrowed. "I never—"

"What?" Cathian stood fast. "This is the first I'm hearing of this."

Raff motioned him to silence, glowering at his uncle. "They got us alone...and proceeded to laugh at how stupid we'd been to trust them. One of them took a liking to my mother, and dragged her into the bedroom. The one left with me said he'd been paid to end *your problem*." He flashed the blade. "He pulled this out and came at me. But I'd already had to kill by that age. He was so cocky, so certain I wouldn't put up a fight."

Raff's voice deepened. "That was a fatal mistake. He died quickly. Then I rushed into the bedroom and took out the second one by jumping on his back. He had my struggling mother pinned under him while he attempted to rip the clothing from her body. It was too easy to slit his throat."

"I don't know what you're talking about!" Beltsen denied.

"There were papers in one of their pockets, Uncle. A contract. An agreement to pay them for killing us—with your signature. I still have it, and I've made copies. Proof that *you* hired killers to take out your own blood. You knew with certainty that I was a Vellar. And you attempted to have us murdered to cover it up forever. You failed."

Beltsen's complexion took on a sickly hue. Rex quickly dropped from sight behind him.

Cathian snarled. "How could you?"

Raff didn't spare his cousin a glance. "This is the last thing I'm going to say to you, so pay close attention. I will *end you* if you continue to fuck with Cathian, his life-lock, or threaten to take *The Vorge* from us. If you try to hire more assassins—and actually send a competent team next time—upon my death, that contract will be released to every ruling family on Tryleskian. I'm certain you've made plenty of enemies. You'll go to prison for the rest of your life.

"Cathian allowing me to make *The Vorge* my home is the only reason you're breathing. You try to take my home away, or fuck with the only Vellar I give a shit about, and *you stop*. Don't ever forget it." He turned away but looked back briefly. "I like Nara. Fuck with her, you fuck with *me*. Make certain no rumors spread...or that contract will, too."

He walked out of view and waited by the door.

"We're done here," Cathian growled. He cut the signal.

"He's afraid," One stated.

"We didn't sense his thoughts. He's too far away," Three murmured. "But it was clear."

"I think I even peed myself a little bit," Two whispered, glancing at Raff. "You are excellent at threats."

Dovis chuckled. "I'm glad you're on our side. I doubt they'll be eager to fuck with us again for a while. If ever."

Raff nodded. "I meant every word. My loyalty is to our family on *The Vorge*. They will never separate us. Not without dying."

His cousin gave him a shattered look. "I had no idea. Why didn't you ever tell me that he sent assassins?"

Raff hesitated. "You're an honorable man, Cathian. When I heard you'd landed on the surface and were looking for me, I thought your father had sent you to try to kill me again. It's why I let you find me so easily. When I was a child, after that happened, my mother and I fled to the desert to hide in a cave for a few years. She feared they'd send more teams after us. I was done hiding and running once I reached adulthood. But you didn't come at me with a blade. You opened your arms and accepted me as your family. You apologized for what had been done to me, and I saw your shame over our fathers' actions. It tortured you. I didn't want to add to your burden of guilt."

"You still should have told me."

Raff sighed. "I didn't see a reason until today. I'm done with their threats and their attempts to control us. It ends now."

Nara approached him, touching his arm gently. "I like you, too. And you're scary as hell, by the way. Thank you. I'm grateful you're part of my family."

He nodded, his gaze locking on Cathian. "It's also time I end my hunt."

"Hunt?" Nara glanced at Cathian, then back to Raff.

"There's one more male responsible for his mother's death, who Raff hasn't found," Two explained. "He hunted down the rest of the group that murdered her. It's all he can do to avenge her death, since taking out his uncle and his father isn't an option. At least not yet...unless they're stupid."

"I'll set a course to Gluttren Four. We have some business to take care of in a system near there. I'd planned to do it next month, but fuck my father's schedules. We're doing things our way from now on." Cathian tapped the controls and glanced at Raff. "How much time do you need?"

"Perhaps a week. But I won't leave the surface until I find the bastard."

"Done. Do you want help? Dovis and I would back you up. York, too, I'm certain."

"This is something I need to do alone." He turned, exiting the bridge.

Raff wished he could kill a couple of Vellars, men who truly deserved it, but he'd settle for the one remaining male who'd been successful in murdering his mother. Vengeance would be his.

Up next…Raff!

About the Author

NY Times and USA Today Bestselling Author

I'm a full-time wife, mother, and author. I've been lucky enough to have spent over two decades with the love of my life and look forward to many, many more years with Mr. Laurann. I'm addicted to iced coffee, the occasional candy bar (or two), and trying to get at least five hours of sleep at night.

I love to write all kinds of stories. I think the best part about writing is the fact that real life is always uncertain, always tossing things at us that we have no control over, but when writing you can make sure there's always a happy ending. I love that about being an author. My favorite part is when I sit down at my computer desk, put on my headphones to listen to loud music to block out everything around me, so I can create worlds in front of me.

For the most up to date information, please visit my website. www.LaurannDohner.com

www.ingramcontent.com/pod-product-compliance
Lightning Source LLC
Chambersburg PA
CBHW020400130626
46549CB00006B/2366